"Why are you staring at me?"

"Sorry," Jordan said. "I was remembering how you looked in your cheerleader costume."

"That was a long time ago. Why did you want to meet with me?"

"To tell you I'm not in the market for a wife."

"What!" Carley glanced around as several people looked curiously at their table. "Surely you don't think that I— Damn!"

Jordan felt a perverse pleasure in having shattered her patina of coolness. "Will you pass the pepper?"

"No! How can you be so self-centered as to think I care anything about you at all?"

He reached across the table and took the pepper shaker from her hand. "If I don't mean anything to you, why are you afraid?"

"Afraid?" Carley stood up so abruptly her chair nearly tipped over. "There's only one reason you aren't *wearing* your lunch home—you aren't worth the effort!"

Dear Reader:

Stellar is the word that comes to mind for this month's array of writers here at Silhouette **Special Edition**.

Launching a gripping, heart-tugging new "miniseries" is dynamic Lindsay McKenna. *A Question of Honor* (#529) is the premiere novel of *LOVE AND GLORY*, celebrating our men (and women!) in uniform and introducing the Trayherns, a military family as proud and colorful as the American flag. Each *LOVE AND GLORY* novel stands alone, but in the coming months you won't want to miss a one—together they create a family experience as passionate and moving as the American Dream.

Not to be missed, either, are the five other stirring Silhouette **Special Edition** novels on the stands this month, by five more experts on matters of the heart: Barbara Faith, Lynda Trent, Debbie Macomber, Tracy Sinclair and Celeste Hamilton.

Many of you write in asking to see more books about characters you met briefly in a Silhouette **Special Edition**, and many of you request more stories by your favorite Silhouette authors. I hope you'll agree that this month—and every month—Silhouette **Special Edition** offers you the stars!

Best wishes,

Leslie J. Kazanjian,
Senior Editor

LYNDA TRENT
Repeat Performance

Silhouette Special Edition

Published by Silhouette Books New York

America's Publisher of Contemporary Romance

SILHOUETTE BOOKS
300 East 42nd St., New York, N.Y. 10017

ISBN: 0-373-09534-1

First Silhouette Books printing June 1989

Books by Lynda Trent

Silhouette Intimate Moments

Designs #36
Taking Chances #68
Castles in the Sand #134

Silhouette Desire

The Enchantment #201
Simple Pleasures #223

Silhouette Special Edition

High Society #378
A Certain Smile #409
Heat Lightning #443
Beguiling Ways #457
Like Strangers #504
Repeat Performance #534

LYNDA TRENT

started writing romances at the insistence of a friend, but it was her husband who provided moral support whenever her resolve flagged. Now husband and wife are both full-time writers of contemporary and historical novels, and despite the ups and downs of this demanding career, they love every—well *almost* every—minute of it.

OKLAHOMA

NEW
MEXICO

ARK.

TEXAS

Fort Worth ● ● Dallas

● Apple Tree

LA.

Austin
★

Houston
●

San Antonio
●

MEXICO

Gulf of Mexico

Underlined places are fictitious.

Chapter One

The tall blond woman crossed the floor and lightly rested one arm on the Styrofoam fireplace. "Once and for all, Robert, I'm here to stay."

The man on the couch sat bolt upright, and the maid gasped as she clutched a silver tray to her chest.

Then the red velvet curtains closed with a swish and the audience enthusiastically applauded. "Robert," who had appeared astounded moments before, frantically pressed his mustache, held in place by spirit gum, as he hurried into the wings.

When everyone was offstage, the curtains were drawn open again and the maid led the cast in a curtain call. As the blond woman, the last of the cast members to take her bow, strode briskly on stage, the audience stood, first in pairs, then in groups, until all were on their feet, applauding wildly.

Carley McKay smiled happily as she glanced toward center stage awaiting the final cue, then followed the blonde's lead as the entire cast simultaneously bowed. Shelley Carstair had starred in so many of the Apple Tree Community Theater shows that she had become an institution. Carley stepped back with the others to allow the curtain to sway shut again.

"This damned mustache nearly fell off in that last scene," the leading man complained. "And it *itches*."

Shelley gave him a distant smile. "I told you to grow a real one."

"My wife hates mustaches." He peeled it off as he headed for the dressing rooms.

Carley removed her maid's cap and ran her fingers through her auburn hair, letting it tumble around her shoulders. The elastic in the cap had given her a headache, and the black shoes she had borrowed from the prop room had cramped her toes. She eased the shoes off and handed them, the cap and her frilly apron to Stacy Rawlins, who was in charge of costumes. "Why do we go through this?" Carley moaned. "Those shoes may have crippled me for life."

"For the *theatre*, my dear," Stacy dramatically replied, mocking the throaty manner of Shelley. Then she laughed. "After a few days' rest you'll be glad to do it again. We all will."

"I know. I think we're all crazy. Can you unbutton me?"

Stacy juggled the shoes to the crook of her elbow and opened the back of Carley's dress. Backstage there were few inhibitions.

"Thanks. I'll bring it up to the prop room as soon as I change."

"I'll be there."

Carley threaded her way down the well-known path between flats and the wall, which had been painted to look like a backyard. The dressing rooms were in the rear of the building where the scenery and larger props were stored. There were doors on the cubicles, but few of the actors ever bothered to close them, and seldom did anyone think anything about it.

"You were great tonight," Carley called out to the leading man as he pulled on his slacks.

"Thanks. So were you. I'm just glad it's over. I haven't talked to my wife or seen my kids since we went into nightly rehearsals."

Carley went into the room she shared with Shelley and began to slip off her dress. Shelley had already changed and was sitting at the vanity. "This one was a big success," Carley said breathlessly. "You're always so good."

Shelley smiled at her. "Thank you. Have you heard what play we do next?"

As Carley tossed her dress over a chair and pulled on her blouse, she said, "I haven't heard."

"Someone said it will be *Moonbeams and Roses*."

"The one Chester Goode wrote?" Carley looked up with interest.

"That's the one. Personally, I think it's a mistake."

Carley made no comment. The female lead called for a young woman. Shelley was nearly forty-five. The story was that of a bittersweet love, with a predictable, though sad, ending. When Carley had read it several months before she had been deeply moved. The story was so similar to her own lost love. She pulled on her jeans and shoved her feet into her moccasin-style loafers. That had all begun so long ago—fifteen years to be exact. A lot had happened to her since then.

"Tryouts are a week from Wednesday," Shelley added.

"So soon?"

"You know Chester. He wants us to have plenty of time to get everything perfect before opening night."

"He's not directing it, is he?"

"No, thank goodness. Bob Holton has agreed to do it. Chester would drive us all crazy."

Bob Holton. Carley thoughtfully brushed her hair back and tied it low on her neck. Bob Holton was the theater's best director, and Carley had been wanting the opportunity to act under his guidance. And she was exactly the right type for the lead. "What time are tryouts?"

"Seven o'clock. Are you auditioning?" Shelley glanced at her in surprise. "That play has no comic relief parts."

"I can play other roles," Carley said firmly, then softened as she realized Shelley had meant no offense. "I guess I'm becoming typecast."

"So am I," Shelley said as she liberally applied cold cream to her face to remove the heavy makeup.

Carley made no comment. There was no problem in being typecast when you were always cast in the role of star. "Will you be there?"

"Maybe. I haven't decided yet."

That meant she would. Carley felt a bit discouraged. If Shelley set foot on stage, she was almost certain to be cast. It happened with regularity.

Carley finished changing quickly and carried her black dress upstairs to the prop room and gave it to Stacy. "Do you want me to help you with these? I could wash some of them at home."

"No. That's okay. But thanks for asking. I'll do it. I have all these others to tend to. I'll just throw them all in together."

"Why don't you ever try out for a part? I think you'd really enjoy it. Acting gets in your blood, you know."

"Me?" Stacy shoved the maid's dress into a bulging laundry bag. "I have no desire to be on stage. I prefer it back here." She gestured at the shelves of vases and chalices and wigs and various hats. "I can find my way around in here blindfolded."

"It's a good thing. None of the rest of us could."

"You haven't removed your makeup. Aren't you going to the cast party?"

"Not this time. I'm exhausted."

"This was a very demanding play. Everyone is worn out."

Carley nodded. "All I want to do is to go home, take a long, hot bath with lots of bubbles and sleep for about a week."

Stacy gave her a searching look. "You aren't feeling lonely and depressed again, are you?"

"No, I'm past that, thank goodness. It was rough for a while after Edward died, but I'm used to the idea now. I still have happy memories of him, and I'm determined not to fall back into that depression."

"I'd be lonely in that big house."

"I have most of the rooms shut off. The part I'm living in really isn't any larger than a small house."

"It's not the same."

"Edward has been gone for a year now. I've put my life back in shape. Actually, I enjoy the privacy. Tonight I'm going to curl up with a copy of the script of *Moonbeams and Roses*. No distractions. No interruptions."

"You're trying out for it? What part?"

"I was considering Alice."

"The lead!"

"You needn't sound all that surprised. Shelley Carstair isn't the only one around here who can play a lead role."

Stacy laughed. "I didn't mean it that way."

"Let's just hope Bob Holton believes it. He's the director."

"Go get in that bathtub. I'm going to close up here and head for the party."

"Have fun for me," Carley said as she went back down the stairs. Normally she wouldn't have missed a cast party, but this play had been unusually tiring. She said goodbye to the other actors, all looking much more ordinary without the heavy stage makeup, and started out of the building.

The theater building had been built in 1885 as an opera house for the performance of live theater, but through the years the structure had housed almost everything from a dentist's office to a department store. The theater group had bought it and restored it to its former Victorian grandeur. Every time Carley walked up the aisles of red velvet seats and looked up at the beautiful, horseshoe-shaped balcony, she felt a thrill at having been a part of it. A large portion of the funds for its restoration had come from her own checking account. At least, she thought wryly, no one could accuse her of buying her way into a lead role. Although she had been in several plays, thus far she had played only bit parts.

The lobby was empty, and the janitor was already starting to clean up after the crowd. Carley told him good-night as she pushed open the etched-glass door and stepped from air-conditioned comfort into the hot night.

June was in full swing, and Apple Tree, Texas, was baking in an unusually severe drought. The verdant rolling hills and lush pasture lands for which this portion of the East Texas piney woods were so well-known for had become as parched as many of the town's now yellow lawns. Even the deep-rooted hardwood trees had been suffering, their leaves hanging limp in the still air.

Apple Tree had received its Texas Main Street Project designation several years before, and through the cooperative efforts of the downtown building owners, the entire downtown area had been rejuvenated. The building fronts had all been restored as closely as possible to the appearance they would have had when they were new. Several blocks of Main Street itself had been replaced by a parklike green. An avenue of elms had been planted along the sidewalks and flowers circled the base of each tree. As a result, the center of town had an old-fashioned charm that was reflected throughout the rest of the community. Carley loved Apple Tree and had lived there all thirty-three years of her life. She had taken the town for granted as a child, moaned as a teenager when in the spirit of modernization the beautiful old building fronts were hidden behind aluminum facades and rejoiced when they reappeared again under the Main Street restoration.

She got in her sleek new Mercedes, and the engine purred obediently to life. There were advantages to having married a wealthy man. The streets were quiet as she drove home. Nightlife was almost nonexistent in Apple Tree.

Her house, only a few blocks from downtown, was one of the town's landmarks, having been designed by

Frank Lloyd Wright. The exterior of the multilevel
house was stark and simple, the sleek lines of its white
slab walls interrupted only occasionally by an outdoor
patio or alcove or a wall fabricated from glass bricks.
Expansive windows on the back and sides filled the
house with natural light during the day and gave her an
unobstructed view of the grounds and privacy from the
street. Edward's father had had it built in the 1930s, just
after his first oil well roared in.

Carley snapped on the light and flooded the room
with brilliance. The walls were pale apricot, and the
soft, sensuously rounded furnishings had been done in
shades of apricot, peach and pale blue with golden accents. A huge painting of a yellow crocus and peach-
hued lilies dominated one wall. The carpet was such a
pale lavender that it seemed almost pink in the sunlight. Following Edward's sudden death of a heart attack at the age of fifty-three, Carley had redecorated the
house in an attempt to fill her empty days. But the activity had not helped much, and Carley had mourned
Edward's passing until Stacy dragged her back to the
theater.

Despite the difference in their ages, Carley and Edward had been happy. It was not a passionate love for
either of them, but Carley had come to him on the rebound from one that had been, and Edward's gentle
love had healed her.

She crossed the silent living room and went up the
stairs to her bedroom. It, too, was surrounding on three
sides by windows, because, like the living room below,
it jutted out into the backyard. Here, also, Carley had
redecorated extensively. Only the art deco four-poster
with its huge lucite bedposts remained. She had replaced the old spread with one of white eyelet lace and

piled pillow shams against the head. Sheer lace panels draped over the brass rods that joined the tops of the bedposts. It was a feminine room and a romantic one. Edward McKay would never have felt comfortable here. But then this had been her room for all the years they had not shared a bedroom. After Edward's death, she had turned his bedroom into a guest room, but it had never been used, since everyone she knew lived right there in Apple Tree.

In her mauve-and-aqua bathroom, Carley undressed before she applied cold cream to remove the thick stage makeup. She considered going to the cast party after all—it would last for hours—but she decided against it. To go there tonight would be tantamount to admitting how lonely she was, and Carley couldn't let herself do that. As she ran water in the big tub, she wiped away the makeup, noting that she looked younger than her years and very vulnerable without it. Her wide brown eyes were soft and dreamy, and her nose still showed a faint hint of freckles. Fourteen years of marriage and a year of widowhood had aged her very little. She was a bit older than Alice, the lead role in *Moonbeams and Roses*, but she was close enough in appearance to pass on stage. She looked more the part than Shelley did.

Turning from the mirror, she stepped into the bubbling bath and slid low until the hot water relaxed all her muscles. She wouldn't think of her loneliness or what might have been, she told herself firmly. She would think about the next play. She closed her eyes and willed her brain to comply.

Jordan Landry was back in town. At first he almost hadn't recognized the downtown area with its fresh paint and renovated shops. The elm trees that had been transplanted during the facelift had turned the formerly utilitarian sidewalks into a pleasant place to stroll. Baedeker's Department Store now bore the sign Opera House and was a theater of some sort. Raintree's Pharmacy had restored the old soda fountain. Everywhere he looked, the town was new and old all at the same time. He had missed Apple Tree. He hadn't seen it for fifteen years.

Most of Jordan's time since his return had been spent settling into the house and organizing the legal practice left to him by his aunt. She had been proud that he had followed in her steps as an attorney, and since she had no children of her own, his aunt had made him her sole heir. When he was first informed of his inheritance, Jordan hadn't been entirely pleased. Both the house and the law practice were located in Apple Tree, and Jordan had never expected to set foot there again.

Soon, however, he realized that owning his own legal practice, plus a graceful old Queen Anne-style house, was preferable to living in his small Houston apartment, fighting rush-hour traffic and being the last name on the door of the law firm. So he had cut his ties—a task he had found surprisingly easy—and moved back to Apple Tree.

He hadn't been there three hours when the company started arriving. In a town the size of Apple Tree no one could sneeze without all the town knowing it. But rather than finding the nonstop attention unsettling, Jordan ate it up. By the time a week had passed, he felt as if he had never left home at all.

Because his aunt had had impeccable taste, he had sold his own furniture before leaving Houston and on his arrival had instructed the movers to put all the boxes of his personal belongings in the bedrooms he wouldn't be using. That way his things wouldn't be underfoot as he decided what to do with his aunt's belongings.

All had gone well with the unpacking and settling in until he came to the last box. He had put this one off until all the others were gone. Kneeling beside it, Jordan carefully opened the top. Inside were the things a boy would love and collect—a baseball glove, a toy train, a stuffed dog, storybooks.

Jordan's eyes stung as he reverently handled the objects that had been meaningful to his son. His son. He never had been certain he was Kevin's biological father, but that hadn't mattered. Jordan had loved him as his own from the day he was born.

He sat back and held Kevin's favorite stuffed dog on his knees. Kevin would have loved this old house and the big backyard that sloped down to the crescent-shaped lake. Kevin would have loved to have grown up.

Too late he realized the track his thoughts were taking, so he replaced the dog in the box and resealed it. He turned his thoughts to his ex-wife instead. Cindy Wallace Landry—or Cindy Lou as she had been called in Apple Tree. He could trace every heartache of his life to that woman. She had stepped between him and his high school sweetheart on a night when he and Carley had argued and temporarily broken up. Then, three months later, Cindy Lou had named him as the father of the baby she was carrying. Carley had vowed never to see him again.

Jordan had done what their parents called "the right thing" and had married her. Cindy Lou had proceeded to make his life miserable for the next eight years. Then one terrible day during one of Houston's freak ice storms, the car in which Cindy and Kevin were riding had slipped off an icy freeway and plunged down an embankment. Kevin died before the ambulance arrived.

Cindy had blamed Jordan for not putting chains on the tires before she needed to leave; he had blamed her for driving on an icy freeway when it wasn't necessary. Within a year of Kevin's death, they were divorced, and a month after that she married one of Jordan's best friends. Jordan had been so glad to see her out of his life that he had only pity for his former friend and a mild curiosity as to how Cindy could have had an affair without him suspecting.

Without Cindy holding him back and spending every cent as fast as he could make it, Jordan went to college and emerged as a lawyer.

Resolutely, he put the box on a shelf in one of the back bedrooms. So much had happened since he had slept here as a boy on weekends. His parents had moved away since then, and their house had been torn down to make room for a new grocery store. The downtown was different now.

And he had not yet caught so much as a glimpse of Carley Kingston.

Jordan closed the closet door. Carley Kingston. What memories the mere thought of her name evoked—luxurious red-brown hair, laughing brown eyes, freckles that danced across her nose. Where was she these days? Probably she had moved away, and certainly she must have married. He wondered if she was happy. The thought that she might not be made him feel uneasy inside. Jordan had known enough unhappiness for them both.

Slowly he walked back through the large house, ruminating over the pros and cons of his decision to move back. His apartment had been small, but the number of steps to get from his bedroom to the front door to answer the doorbell had been far fewer than in this huge house. Here he no longer had to contend with the nightmarish traffic, but he would miss the abundance of speciality stores within only a few miles of home, and that would take some getting used to. He was looking forward to owning his legal practice and not having to answer to a boss or having to struggle his way up the corporate ladder, but just as the town was smaller, so were its problems. The biggest challenge he had to face that day was the legal entanglement of Joe Fisher's Angus bull having impregnated Harry Dunlap's registered Hereford. He couldn't recall a single case of that sort in the records of Bushman, Harcourt and Graves in downtown Houston.

Still feeling somewhat edgy, he went downstairs to the living room to look for something to occupy his time. Aunt Estelle had enjoyed comfort, and all the furniture was big and overstuffed. The room had two bay windows, one overlooking the front yard, the other the attached summer house, which was really an extension off the porch. Both were sunny nooks for reading or daydreaming, with cushioned window seats and overhanging arches of white gingerbread. A matching arch topped the double doors that opened onto the dining room. Overhead hung an elaborate crystal chandelier. The first week Jordan was in the house, he painted the living room walls a deep blue, which complemented the blue-and-white chintz of the furniture and saved the room from being old-fashioned. Jordan felt more at ease here than anywhere in the house, perhaps because he'd given some of himself to it.

He lowered himself onto the couch and opened the newspaper. There wasn't much to read—the local daily was only ten pages or so, containing mostly sale and want ads, a few news wire stories and an item or two of local interest such as which boy's calf had placed first in the recent FFA judging. Apple Tree had no movie theater, though the grocery store rented videos. Jordan would have said he wasn't the sort to need an active nightlife, but he was quickly realizing that Apple Tree had no nightlife at all.

A small article, buried between Winifred Parson's squash casserole recipe and Frank Winchell's tractor advertisement, caught Jordan's eye. This was the second and last night of tryouts for a play called *Moonbeams and Roses*. He had never heard of the play, but he had done some acting in one of the neighborhood theaters in Houston. On the spur of the moment he decided to go down and read for a part.

Carley sat on the couch that had been used in the last play. Several actors were scattered around the set on folding chairs or sitting on the edge of the stage. Although the auditorium was only dimly lit, she could see Chester Goode pacing up and down the aisle. Chester had written this play as he had several others, but none of them had ever been performed outside Apple Tree, nor were they likely ever to be. He was a newcomer by Apple Tree standards, having lived there only twenty-three years. Chester was on the far side of middle age and was as nervous as a terrier. He moved in jerky motions and had run his bony fingers through his hair until it stood up in gray peaks. Carley always worried about Chester's health when one of his plays was performed because his nervousness increased to a frenzied pitch by opening night.

The director, Bob Holton, was Chester's exact opposite. Although Bob looked like a football coach, he earned his living as an electrician and had never been known to raise his voice or to get unduly upset—except for the time Becky Jean Morley had had trouble memorizing her lines and had written them on every prop on the stage. Bob had a knack for making Chester feel included by asking his opinion, then ignoring it in such a way that Chester thought things were being done his way. Chester had often said Bob Holton was the only man in town he could work with.

Carley sat back and watched as Shelley Carstair read for the part of Alice. When Chester's face brightened, she told herself there was no reason for the rest of them to be there. Shelley always got the lead role.

Carley glanced around the room. Not many men had come to read on either night. Most of the actors were still exhausted from the last play, which had called for a big cast, and several were on vacation or at Little League games. There wasn't a single person there who was right for Buck, the male lead.

"Carley," Bob said, "this time you read the part of Alice. The rest of you continue as you were. Let's begin on page sixteen with Alice's line, 'Surely I haven't.'"

She stood and flipped through the script to the right page. She knew this scene. It was the one where Alice first told Buck that she wanted more in life than her parents had. Drawing a steadying breath, Carley started to speak, putting herself aside and letting the magic of the stage take over. For a few brief moments she became Alice, a woman of quick intelligence who was seemingly doomed to a mundane life. Her clear voice rang across the empty auditorium, sounding like that of a woman desperately striving to make her fiancé see that she dreamed of more than housework and overdue bills.

"That's good," Bob broke in, his tone noncommittal. "Melissa, read the part of the mother on page twenty-eight."

Carley went back to the couch, her heart racing with the exhilaration she felt from having done a good reading, yet she knew she shouldn't get her hopes up. Forcing herself, she turned her full attention to the reading in progress. Melissa Thompson had a natural gift of mimicry, which made her an excellent character actress. She could convince an audience she was any age from fifteen to fifty.

As Carley struggled to keep her attention on Melissa by following the script, she noticed the door at the back of the auditorium open, casting a wedge of light down the dim aisle. For a moment a man was silhouetted in the doorway, his shoulders broad, his hips narrow. Her pulse quickened. There was something so familiar about the way he carried himself.

The door swung shut with a click that was clearly audible in the echoing auditorium. Melissa continued reading, but Carley's attention was solely on the man. Although his outline was vague in the room's shadows, she could see that he moved with the lithe grace of an athlete. As he approached the lighted stage, Carley's eyes widened. It couldn't be! Not after all these years!

"That's enough, Melissa," Bob said, then swiveled to look up at the newcomer.

"Sorry I'm late." Even though the man spoke softly, his mellow voice carried well, seeming to resonate at the center of Carley's being. "I just found out about the tryouts. Am I too late to read for a part?"

Bob's face lit up in a grin that was echoed by Chester's. "Not at all. I'm Bob Holton, the director. This is our playwright, Chester Goode."

"I'm Jordan Landry."

A trembling, which started in Carley's middle, quickly spread down to her toes. Her legs went rubbery and her fingers were like ice. His voice, so clearly remembered, was a bit deeper, the cadence more calm, but it was his voice.

Jordan came up the steps and onto the stage, the front spots accentuating the ruddy highlights in his dark brown hair. His eyes appeared silver. At the edge of the set he paused, and his gaze met Carley's.

She couldn't move, and she couldn't have spoken if her life had depended on it. The years disappeared, and it was as if her marriage and widowhood had been nothing but a fantasy. In the mesmerizing silver of his eyes, even the stage and the people upon it faded. Jordan Landry was back in town.

"Somebody give him a book," Bob said as Chester perched on the edge of a seat. "Start reading on page seventeen where Buck says, 'Alice, you can't mean.' Carley, read Alice's part."

She wasn't sure how she managed to stand and walk to the center of the stage. She felt light-headed and suddenly shy. She wanted to run—but she wasn't sure whether she would run to him or away from him.

"Hello, Carley," he said quietly when they stood face-to-face.

"Jordan," she replied, as if his mere name were greeting enough after fifteen years.

His face was more mature. The fine lines that fanned from the corners of his eyes and bracketed his mouth only enhanced his charisma. Jordan had always been the sexiest man she had ever seen.

"Well?" Bob prompted.

Jordan gave her another soul-searching look, then raised the script and began to read.

Carley was sure her voice would crack or that she would stumble over the lines, but that wasn't the case. Her responses to Jordan's lines held a ring of truth, probably, she thought, because she had once said more or less the same things to him so long ago.

Out of the corner of her eye, she saw Chester resume his pacing, his movements as sharp and jerky as a sparrow's. She was all too aware of the words she was reading, and for the first time she actually became Alice. The other actors, Bob and Chester disappeared, and she was Alice trying to explain her dreams to Buck, who only wanted to give her the security of a home and family.

When the reading ended, Carley was glaring up at Jordan with such an intensity that for a moment she was embarrassed. Then his eyes softened, and she hastily stepped back and looked away.

"Good, good, good," Chester chirped as he characteristically wrung his hands. "Marvelous!"

"That's it for tonight," Bob said as he scrawled notes on his legal pad. "I'll call you all in a day or two to let you know how I've cast this. Rehearsal will start next Tuesday at seven sharp."

Whereas Carley had been unable to tear her eyes from Jordan before, she now studiously avoided looking at him at all. She was afraid of the reaction she'd had to his voice, the faint scent of his cologne, and especially his eyes. If she gazed into his eyes again, she might never want to look away.

"Carley?" he said.

She pretended not to hear and all but ran from the stage.

All the way home she cursed her luck and whatever star had drawn him back to Apple Tree. For fifteen years she had tried to forget Jordan Landry, and she thought she had succeeded. She had believed he would no longer have such an earth-shattering effect on her. But then she had also believed she would never see him again.

When she was safely at home with her door locked and the lights on, she tried to summon the anger his image usually evoked, but seeing him again so unexpectedly had confused her. He had jilted her to marry Cindy Lou Wallace, and they had had a baby only seven months later. By his own admission he had slept with Cindy Lou while he was supposedly going steady with Carley. While he was professing love for her, he had to have been making love with Cindy Lou on the side, a girl with a reputation for being easy.

Carley turned on the television and stared at the screen, but her thoughts were on Jordan. He had no right to return to Apple Tree and to come back into her world! He had no right to barge into tryouts and read for the part of Buck when she was reading for Alice. And he had no right to look so sexy and provocative and tempting.

Carley slid lower in her chair and hugged a pale blue throw pillow to her stomach. After the way he had treated her, how could he be so damned desirable? Couldn't he at least have the decency to look jaded? The sound of her name on his lips had turned her insides to jelly. And where was his wife?

The thought of Cindy Lou sparked the anger Carley sought. Jordan's wife. She would doubtless come to watch rehearsals, and that would be intolerable!

With trembling fingers, Carley dialed Bob Holton's number. She would take her name off the tryout list. Maybe she would take a long vacation...to Europe. Perhaps by the time she returned Jordan and his wife would have tired of Apple Tree and moved back to wherever they came from. "Hello, Bob? This is Carley."

"Carley! What a coincidence. I was just trying to decide if it was too late to call you. I'm putting you in the role of Alice."

She gripped the receiver tightly. The lead role? She had never been given a lead before. And this was a part she had wanted so much!

"Carley? Are you there?"

"Yes. Alice, you say? You want me and not Shelley?"

"She's not right for this part. I pictured you in it all along."

"You did?" Her mouth felt like cotton, but she forced herself to ask, "Who will you cast as Buck?"

"Jordan Landry, of course. How could I even consider anyone else? He *is* Buck. I thought Chester was going to chew his fingernails up to his elbow before I told him Jordan has the part."

"I see. Bob, I'm not sure I'm the one to do this. You see—"

"Nonsense. Of course you are. If you had been sitting where I was and had seen the electricity between you two, you wouldn't have a single doubt."

Electricity, she thought, was a mild term for the sparks Jordan had always engendered within her. "But—"

"No buts about it. You two are perfect. Besides, everybody is tired of seeing Shelley in the lead role. She's good, but so are you. I'm casting Melissa as your mother. We'll have to age her, of course, but that's not difficult."

Carley pretended to listen as Bob ran through the rest of the cast. The good news, she thought almost hysterically, was that she got the lead; the bad news was that Jordan did, too. The goods news was that Jordan Landry was back in town; the bad news was that Jordan Landry was back in town.

After she hung up the phone, Carley stared sightlessly at the television. No matter how he affected her, she wasn't going to let him get close to her again. Perhaps she couldn't avoid him at the theater, but that didn't mean she had to see him and his wife socially. She wished with all her heart that Edward was still alive to act as her buffer against the world. Edward had given her security with a capital *S*; Jordan was like a roller coaster ride with all the switches full open.

Yes, she decided, she would avoid Jordan Landry at all costs.

Chapter Two

By the following Tuesday Carley had her world back in perspective. She was no longer Carley Kingston who had been vulnerable and shy and who wore her heart on her sleeve. She was Carley McKay, the respected widow of the richest man in town and one who was secure in the knowledge of her own worth. She arrived at rehearsal wearing a brick-red silk blouse and white slacks. A double rope of fine gold chain circled below her lapels, and she wore a gold nugget ring on her right hand. If anyone had asked her, Carley would have flatly denied that she had taken such care to dress for Jordan.

She breezed into the theater with as much confidence as if she owned this building, as she did many of the others in town. Stacy and Melissa were sitting in the front row and conferring over Melissa's costume. Carley joined them and glanced at the sketches Stacy had made.

"I'm glad you were cast as Alice," Melissa said. She brushed her wispy blond hair back and smiled at Carley. Offstage Melissa had none of the presence she brought to her roles. She seemed childlike in her sweetness and was in the process of divorcing her husband.

"How are you, Melissa? Is everything going smoothly?"

"With Jack, you mean? Not smoothly at all, I'm afraid. He's trying to convince me to give him another chance."

"You aren't considering it, are you?" Stacy asked in a low voice. "He put you in the hospital the last time!"

Melissa lowered her large blue eyes. "I know. When's he's not drinking, he's not so bad, though. And I really am lonesome without him."

"Get a puppy to talk to," Stacy advised. "You aren't a punching bag."

Carley saw the tears gather in Melissa's eyes and said, "I hear this time is the most difficult in getting a divorce. Once it's final, you won't be under so much pressure."

Melissa nodded. "I know you're right. I don't want to go back to Jack. He frightens me. Sometimes I wonder how I got the nerve to file against him."

"The important thing is that you did it," Stacy said.

Melissa's eyes grew wide. "Estelle Landry was the lawyer who helped me file, but now that she's dead, I don't know where that leaves me."

"I've heard her nephew has taken over all her cases," Stacy said as she made a few corrections on her sketches.

"He was here for the last night of tryouts," Melissa said in her whispery voice. "I couldn't take my eyes off him! And you get to play opposite him, Carley. I wish I were Alice instead of her mother."

"I wish you were, too," Carley said wryly. "I'm not looking forward to this."

"Why on earth not?" Stacy demanded. "I think he's the best-looking man Apple Tree has ever seen."

Carley shrugged. Both Stacy and Melissa had moved to town after Jordan had left. Neither of them knew of her connection with him, and Carley preferred it that way.

"Look," Melissa murmured, "here he comes."

Carley didn't need to be told. She had sensed his presence without turning her head. She had always had an instinctive radar where Jordan Landry was concerned. Slowly she turned and was again struck by his magnetism. When their eyes met, he smiled, but she didn't.

Apparently paying no heed to her slight, he joined them. Carley managed to introduce him to Stacy and Melissa, though after so many years his name felt strange in her mouth, almost as if she were speaking the name of someone long dead. But Jordan was most definitely alive, and even Stacy, who was quite happily married, was staring at him as if she would like to take a bite out of him.

"Could I talk to you a minute, Carley?" he was saying.

She could only nod. Anything else would be too obvious. Besides, she told herself, they would have to speak often before the play was over. She tried to look at him as if he were only a casual acquaintance.

When they were in the wings, Jordan stopped walking, and Carley had no choice but to halt as well. "I had hoped to talk to you before now," he said, "but you were in such a hurry to leave tryouts that I couldn't catch you and there are no Kingstons listed in the phone book.''

"My last name is McKay now. What did you want to talk to me about?''

Jordan gazed thoughtfully at her. "Nothing in particular.''

She pretended to be interested in the pulley system that was used to raise and lower the various curtains. "I suppose you're getting settled into your aunt's house.''

"Yes, I am.''

Drawing a steadying breath, Carley added, "I guess Cindy Lou is glad to be back home.''

"Cindy and I are divorced.''

Carley's head snapped up and her eyes widened before she regained control. "Oh? I'm sorry to hear that.''

"I'm surprised that you didn't know.''

"She and I have no friends in common. Her parents moved away soon after yours did, of course.''

"I meant I'm surprised you haven't heard since I returned. Half of Apple Tree has come by to see me.''

"I've been busy at home and down here at the theater. I haven't seen many people.''

He looked at her as if he were memorizing her features, and Carley wondered if she had changed as little as he had. "What about you? Did you marry anyone I know? I can't place anyone named McKay except for Arthur." He laughed and added, "You couldn't have married him." Then he realized she might have and said, "You didn't, did you?''

"No,'' she said frostily. "I didn't. I married Edward McKay.''

"Edward,'' Jordan said thoughtfully. "I don't remember anyone named Edward.''

"Of course you do. He was the president of the bank where Dad worked and was Arthur's father." She had never seen Jordan look so stunned.

"You don't mean . . . But he's as old as . . . You married him?"

"Keep your voice down. Yes, I did, and we were very happy together."

"Were?"

"Edward died last year. It was a heart attack and was quite sudden."

Jordan could only stare at her. "Why in the hell would you marry a man who was old enough to be your father?"

"I loved him!" she snapped. "And I could trust him!"

"His money couldn't have been much of a drawback, either!"

Carley pulled away from him as if he were a snake. "I didn't marry Edward for his money!"

"No?"

"No! And he didn't get me pregnant beforehand!" She was pleased to see the barb sink in. She had wanted to say that to Jordan for fifteen years.

"Everyone on stage for act one," Bob Holton called. "Let's get started."

"That was a low blow," Jordan growled at her.

"Not as low as what you did to me!" she retorted.

"You might try to see it from my point of view. Our parents didn't give us much choice in the matter."

"Sure. I'm really sympathetic toward you, all right. Naturally you never laid a hand on her. Right?" Acid dripped from her words, and her eyes crackled with anger.

"I never said that," he retorted.

Carley felt as though she'd been stabbed. She had expected him to deny it, to say he had been falsely accused and railroaded into marrying Cindy Lou. Jordan was as deceitful and low as she had thought for all those years.

"Since you hadn't heard about my divorce, you probably don't know about Kevin."

"Kevin?" she asked coldly.

"My son. He died when he was seven."

"Oh, no, Jordan!" She was shocked out of her anger.

"It was in a car wreck. The divorce came about soon after."

"I'm so sorry. I had no idea!" She put out her hand as if to touch him, then pulled it back.

"I just wanted you to know."

Jordan brushed past her to go onstage. Forcing all emotion from her face, Carley followed him and took a pencil from the jar at the edge of the footlights. As Bob blocked the action of the play, she wrote notes in the margin of her script, but her thoughts were on what Jordan had said. For some reason she felt guilty for her anger at him now that she knew his son was dead. Perversely this made her even more irate that he made her feel this way.

Each time she had to go near Jordan, she felt her resentment grow. Every time she had to mouth Alice's profession of love to Buck, she felt as if she would choke. When Bob blocked the scene where Carley had to embrace Jordan, she had to fight her desire to slap him. Carley dreaded the time when she would have to not only put her arms around Jordan, but kiss him and say she loved him, too. At the moment she would prefer to scratch his eyes out.

By noon the next day the *Apple Tree Tribune* had published the names of the cast members for *Moonbeams and Roses*, along with a photo of Carley and Jordan in the second act. Carley could almost trace the paper boy's route by the phone calls she received. Everyone congratulated her on being cast in the lead, but it was obvious that everyone was curious about how she felt to be cast opposite Jordan Landry. Life moved slowly in Apple Tree, and memories were long. Almost everybody in town recalled that she and Jordan had planned to marry and why they hadn't.

"No, Mrs. Harding," Carley said for what seemed to be the hundredth time, "Jordan and I aren't dating. No, it's only a play." Her patience was wearing thin, and it was all she could do to answer the woman's questions politely. "Yes, he was a nice-looking boy in high school. Yes, I'm sure his parents are pleased over the way he turned out."

The muted chimes of her doorbell sounded, and Carley uncurled from the couch. "Mrs. Harding, someone is at my door. I have to go now. No, I doubt that it will be Jordan. Yes. Yes, I'll do that." As she tried to extricate herself from the phone, she bent near the side table as she edged around the couch. "Yes, ma'am. I'll tell him when I see him. Yes. Goodbye."

With relief she hung up and hurried to the front door. A quick glance through the peep hole brought a groan to her lips. Forcing herself to smile, Carley swung open the door. "Arthur. How good to see you."

"I've read the paper," her stepson snapped as he brushed past her.

"Come in, Arthur, and make yourself at home," she said to his back.

Arthur was older than Carley by five years, and his hair was thinning as fast as his waist was thickening. He had resented her marriage to his father, though for appearance' sake he visited her regularly.

"Isn't Betsy with you?"

"She had to drop Rosalie at twirling lessons and Eddie at baseball practice."

Carley followed him into the den. "I would have come to Eddie's game last night, but I had play rehearsal."

"I know. That's what I want to talk to you about. Carley, you've got to stop spending so much time at the theater."

"I do? Why?" She sat on the arm of a chair across from where Arthur was pacing.

"Everybody I know has called to tell me that you have the lead role."

"So?"

"It doesn't look right for Edward McKay's widow to play a romantic part in a play! It was bad enough for you to have bit parts, but this is insupportable!"

Carley laughed and slid down into the chair with her knees over the arm. "Give me a break, Arthur. Who cares if I'm in a play? What difference can it possible make?"

"It matters to me! You never acted like this while Dad was alive."

"I was considerably busier then. We were always going places and doing things together. The theater helps me pass the time."

"What about this role you're playing? What about Jordan Landry?"

"What about him?" she asked with convincing casualness.

"You two used to date each other. You nearly married him!"

"Everybody is making a mountain out of a molehill over that. Sure, we dated, but that was way back in high school." She made it sound as if that had been eons ago. "You used to date Barbara Howard, and nobody thinks anything about you shopping in her store."

"I wasn't engaged to Barbara, and I don't act in plays where I have to put my arms around her!"

"Is that what all this is about?" she asked innocently.

"I know you're still young and that in time you may start to date again. I can accept that."

"That's big of you." She was trying hard not to laugh at him.

"But I can't accept you acting like...his *lover* onstage. It's disgraceful!"

She sighed. "Oh, Arthur, you're always so proper. You married the girl your parents wanted you to marry, you had two kids, one of each sex. Eddie plays all the sports, Rosalie takes all the right lessons and they are always on the honor role. You even named your children after your parents! Don't you ever have the slightest temptation to jump naked and howl at the moon?"

"Carley!"

"It's just a figure of speech. If you turn any redder, you'll burst a blood vessel. It's no longer fashionable to close widows away in a nunnery. You live in the wrong century. You would have made a dandy Victorian."

"I gather that means you won't drop out of the play?"

"You gather correctly."

Arthur frowned at her. "I suppose you know I was against Dad marrying you. I always felt you were too young for him. I'm just glad he can't see how you're turning out."

"What an unkind thing to say!" Carley got to her feet and glared at him. "I made your father quite happy."

"You never took the place of my mother," he answered scathingly.

"I never thought that I did! Good heavens, that was altogether different!"

They frowned at each other until Arthur finally drew himself up and said stiffly, "I apologize. That was wrong of me."

"I agree. Arthur, I know you don't especially like me, but you wouldn't have welcomed anyone for a stepmother."

"It would have been considerably easier if my stepmother were older than I am."

"I know. I told Edward that at the time, but you remember how he was. Once he got his mind set on something, he never gave it up."

"How well I know that!"

"But that's neither here nor there. Edward is gone, and I had to get my life back in gear. The theater has helped me to do that."

"And Jordan?"

"I never expected him to move back here, let alone try out for the part of Buck. He was never involved in plays in school."

"People are saying you're interested in him again."

"It's not true. Arthur, I give you my word that Jordan Landry could drop off the earth and I wouldn't care."

Arthur frowned and pursed his lips the way he always did when he was thinking. "I still say it doesn't look right."

"If anybody tells you there is something between Jordan and myself, you just tell them that they're wrong. It's as simple as that." When he looked unconvinced, she said, "There really isn't."

"Well, it's not just me," he said awkwardly. "Betsy is upset, too."

She would be, Carley thought. Betsy spent a great deal of energy doing the right things in life. Aloud Carley said, "You have my word on it, and I should know."

"All right. I'll tell her to squash any rumors she may hear."

"Arthur, it's only a play, for pete's sake. I'm not opening a bordello!"

"Your choice of words is unsettling."

She sighed. "If Edward had acted as old as you do, we would never have gotten together at all. Go watch Eddie's ball practice and quit worrying. I can take care of myself."

"I still say you ought to quit the theater."

"Absolutely not. The play has already gone into rehearsal. I won't do any such thing."

"All right. But I want you to know that I object as the head of the family."

"Arthur, get out of here," Carley said with a laugh. "Head of the family, indeed!"

He glared at her, but he left.

Carley closed the door behind him. Arthur was a pain in the rear, but he had only voiced what everyone else had all day. The phone began ringing again, and this time Carley ignored it. She was tired of explaining.

When the ringing finally quit, Carley dialled the number listed for Estelle Landry. As much as she would prefer not to talk to Jordan, she had to be certain that he knew there was no future for them.

"Jordan? This is Carley McKay." Dumb, she thought. How many Carley's could he know?

There was a pause. "Yes?"

"I was wondering if you would meet me for lunch at Carver House today."

"Carver House?"

"I forget the town has changed since you were here last. It's the old Elias Carver home over on North Main. It's been turned into a restaurant."

Again there was a pause. "Yes," he finally said. "Yes, I could do that."

Carley wondered if the silence meant he was reading more into the invitation than she intended, or if he had merely been checking his day's appointments. "What time is convenient for you?"

"How about noon?"

"Perfect. I'll meet you there. Bye." She hung up and stared incredulously at the phone. She had actually asked Jordan to meet her for lunch! Had she made a mistake? Even after all he had put her through, she couldn't speak to him without having a physical reaction.

Stop it! she chided herself. She hadn't asked him for a romantic date, but rather wanted to set matters straight. Why, she wouldn't go out with Jordan Landry if he begged her. The only purpose for this lunch was so she could be certain that he didn't start getting any ideas that she would be receptive to an advance from him.

A glance at her watch told Carley she had time to wash her hair if she hurried. She wanted to look her best when she told him he didn't have a chance with her.

Jordan had no trouble finding Carley in the restaurant; her auburn hair drew him like a beacon. Since she had called that morning, he had wondered about this meeting. A restaurant seemed an unlikely place for them to go over their lines for the play, and that left only one other reason. Carley must want to resume their relationship where they had left off.

That put Jordan in an uncomfortable position. Fifteen years had passed, and he wasn't the same boy who had been pressured into marrying Cindy and certainly wasn't eager to marry again. If he had learned nothing else from his eight years of hell with Cindy, he knew marriage wasn't all smiles and roses. And since then he had developed no illusions about marriage to someone else being a desirable state. He had been amazed that Carley had married Edward McKay's fortune; he had been convinced that love was more important to her than money. Carley had always been a romantic, and he had to set her straight before she got some sort of romantic notion about him. Perhaps she already had. Quite a few people in town seemed to think so; his phone had rung off the wall all morning with congratulations that he and Carley were back together again. None of them seemed willing to accept that this was only a play, and more than once he'd thought about pulling out. But Jordan was not a quitter. His father had seen to that with his admonition that Jordan should never start anything he didn't intend to finish. The axiom had become a part of his personality.

Carley looked up as he pulled out the chair to be seated. She had chosen a table near a window, and in the sunlight her skin seemed translucent; he noticed a golden hue in her brown eyes that he'd never seen before. She might be a few years older, he observed, but she was more beautiful as a woman than she had been as a girl.

"You're late. I was wondering if you were still coming," she said rather rapidly.

He wasn't sure whether she was upset over something or just in a hurry. "I'm on time. Your watch must be fast." Whatever happened to hello, he wondered.

Jordan waited until after the waitress took their order before he smiled at Carley. "My phone hasn't stopped ringing all morning. I feel as if I landed a part on Broadway."

"I've had several calls, too."

Jordan studied her as he wondered how to tell her he would like her for a friend but nothing else. She was so poised and sophisticated. The Carley he had known was full of spontaneous vitality and bubbling laughter.

"Why are you staring at me?"

"Sorry," he said. "I was remembering how you looked in your cheerleader costume."

"That was a long time ago."

"Yes, it was."

She raised her eyes up to meet his, then glanced away. "I wanted to talk to you about the play."

"Oh? What about it?" Here it comes, he thought. The let's-pick-up-the-pieces-and-go-again ploy.

"I think you should drop out of it."

"What?" He leaned forward.

"No one will think less of you at this point. You can say you're too busy from the move and with your new law practice."

"Why would I say that?"

"Surely you can see that we can't be cast opposite each other in this play. Everybody in town is talking about us!"

"Then *you* drop out."

"Me!"

"And since when have you become so concerned about what people will think?"

"I don't enjoy being the subject of gossip and speculation," she said in a tense voice after glancing around to see if they could be overheard.

"Over being in a play together?" he said with a laugh, though he was well aware of what she meant. "Give me a break!"

"Maybe that would be ridiculous in a city, but not here. You know how Apple Tree is."

"I assumed it had changed." He hadn't intended to provoke her, but couldn't seem to stop.

"That's because you haven't been here."

"Have you? Been here all the time, I mean?" He watched as temper colored her cheeks. "Didn't you go to college?"

"No."

"But you had a scholarship."

She lifted her chin defiantly. "I got married instead."

"One doesn't exclude the other. McKay could afford to send you to college." His words were clipped, and he felt as tense as if she were still married to the man.

"As Edward's wife I didn't need a college degree," she answered haughtily.

Jordan frowned. "Obviously. After all, what good is a degree unless you have to earn a living?" Anger was unaccountably building in him.

"You make it sound as if I only married him for his money! I told you we married for love!"

"Every time we've spoken, you've told me that," he retorted. "Maybe you're protesting a bit too much!"

She closed her lips firmly as the waitress brought their food to the table. As soon as they were alone again, Carley said, "I didn't ask you here to argue. I wanted to tell you that no one will think less of you if you drop out of the play."

"I have no intention of doing any such thing."

"Surely you can see why you can't perform on stage as my lover!"

"If the idea bothers you, then you drop out."

"And have it look as if I couldn't handle being on stage with you?"

"There you go on appearances again. You'll notice *I* didn't come here to demand that *you* quit the play."

"Then why did you agree to meet me?"

"I wanted to tell you that I'm not in the market for a wife."

"What!" She glanced around as several people looked curiously at their table. "Surely you don't think that I . . . I would ever . . . Damn!"

Jordan felt a perverse pleasure at having shattered her patina of coolness. "Will you pass the pepper?"

"No!" Carley leaned forward, her eyes sparking with anger. "How can you be so self-centered as to think I care anything about you at all?"

He reached across the table and took the pepper shaker from her hand. "If I don't mean anything to you, why are you afraid to play Alice?"

"Afraid!" Her voice squeaked in her effort not to scream. "I'm not afraid!"

"Then don't drop out. You'll probably do just fine in the role."

"Don't you dare be condescending to me! Since when are you such an expert actor? You didn't even take speech in high school!"

"You've remembered my curriculum all these years? Touching."

Carley couldn't recall having been this angry since Jordan had left town. "Don't you worry about whether I can play Alice. You just try to be passable as Buck!"

"I can play Buck with my eyes closed."

"We'll just see about that!"

"What an original comeback. Did you pick that up from a comic strip?"

It was all she could do to refrain from dumping her plateful of food over his head.

"Look, I said I didn't come here to argue."

"You couldn't tell it from the way you're behaving!"

"If you'll stop glaring at me for a moment, you'll notice we've become the interest of everyone in here. It doesn't matter to me, but since you've become so socially conscious, I thought I should tell you."

Carley's face flushed red as she realized it was true. All the years of effort she had expended to become accepted in Edward's social circle had been burst like a soap bubble after a few minutes of conversation with Jordan. "Did you come back to town for the express purpose of destroying my life, or is this just a natural by-product of your existence?'' she hissed.

''You didn't get this upset until I told you that I don't want to be romantically involved with you. I guess I should have been more tactful.''

''You don't know beans about romance!''

''I'll bet I know a damned sight more than that old man you married,'' he snapped back.

Carley stood up so abruptly that her chair scraped the floor. Now everyone in the restaurant was unabashedly staring at them. ''There's only one reason you aren't wearing your lunch home—you aren't worth the effort!''

She jerked up her chin as she stalked out, trying hard to ignore Jordan's chuckle. At the register the waitress said, ''Should I have made out two checks, Mrs McKay?''

Carley glared back at Jordan as she reached in her purse for her wallet. ''I'm sure this will cover it all,'' she said as she shoved a large bill across the counter, pleased to see the maddening grin leave Jordan's face. Edward's money did have its advantages.

Chapter Three

Despite Chester Goode's innocuousness as a person, the manner in which he had written his musical, *Moonbeams and Roses*, showed that he had the soul of a true romantic. The melodies for his songs were adaptations of well-known favorites, but the lyrics, tender and yearning with love, were his own. Carley, who had sung in her church choir for years, was confident of her own musical ability, and though Bob Horton had assured her that Jordan could sing, she had been skeptical that they would be well matched for the duets. But she had been wrong. As he began to sing the first love song, she was amazed to discover his voice was as true and as musical as if he had been trained to sing professionally. Carley could have sworn she'd known everything there was to know about Jordan Landry.

On cue her voice blended with his, and their eyes met and held. Despite the gentle words of love that she sang, she wanted to boil him in oil. By the look in his eyes, he felt exactly the same way about her. Their voices lifted and melded in harmony for the length of the song, but as soon as it was ended, both abruptly turned away.

"That's good, that's really good," Chester said gleefully.

"I want you two holding hands on the second verse," Bob directed. "Jordan, by the end, have your arms around her."

Jordan threw her a withering glance. "Okay, Bob."

Bob went back to the piano and nodded at the accompanist. "Carley, let's run through the last verse one more time."

She nodded. How was she ever going to get through this play? She and Jordan were on stage together in virtually every scene. As the woman at the piano began to play, Carley lifted her voice. From the corner of her eye she could see Jordan watching her, and this made her unreasonably nervous. The words to the song flew out of her head, and she faltered and stopped. "I'm sorry. Could we try it again?"

As she resumed, she saw Melissa go to Jordan and whisper something to him. He bent slightly in a way he had of making every word seem important and listened intently. Then he nodded, and they stepped back into the wings. For some reason Carley felt a stab of jealousy.

"That's better," Bob said. "I like that extra fire you added at the end. Do it that way every time."

Carley nodded, hoping she could recall what she had done that was different from before. Her mind had been on Jordan and Melissa.

"Okay, folks, let's run through act three," Bob called out.

She turned to the correct page and positioned herself by the couch. Jordan crossed to the fireplace, and Melissa took her place in the rocker. Carley was thankful they were still using their scripts so she could avoid having to make sustained eye contact with Jordan.

Melissa gave her first line, and Jordan made the proper response. All Carley's attention had to be centered on the action of the play, and she tried to lose herself in Alice's struggle to decide on her future.

In time Jordan and Melissa exited, and Carley sang the solo in which Alice weighed her life as Buck's wife against the glamour of a career of her own. The tune was a difficult one with words that tumbled like bubbling water. The chorus was sung more sedately with words that were bittersweet. Carley had so much trouble following the tune and the words that she couldn't think of Jordan at all.

Somehow she managed to get through the song and the last scene. She especially enjoyed the ending of the play, because in it Alice told Buck she was choosing a career over marriage with him and that he didn't offer her enough incentive for her to give up everything for him. It was this scene that had endeared the play to her in the first place. Carley liked the idea of being the one to break a heart, especially now that Jordan was cast as Buck.

When she exited stage left through what would eventually be the front door, Carley felt better. Maybe it was worth the love songs to be able to leave Jordan in front of an entire audience and hear their applause when she did.

As usual the cast came back on stage for Bob's critiques and comments, and Carley dutifully readied her pencil to mark his recommended changes in her script.

"Page forty-one. Alice and Buck. I want a kiss here."

"What?" they asked in unison.

"A kiss. You're supposed to be lovers. You just sang a love song. I want this act to end with a kiss." Bob looked from Carley on one end of the set to Jordan on the other. "You don't have a problem with that, do you?"

"Not me," Jordan said rather grimly.

"I guess not," Carley said coolly.

"Good. And I don't want a stage kiss, either. With our audience so close to the stage, they can tell the difference."

Carley frowned at her script. A kiss! And one long enough to bring down the curtain! She felt a stirring that she immediately labeled as distaste. Certainly the idea of kissing Jordan held no enticement for her!

Bob finished his comments and instructions and dismissed them. Carley made a point of keeping her back to Jordan, and he made no effort to speak to her.

"Aren't you the lucky one!" Melissa murmured as she and Carley left the stage.

"Me? In what way?" Carley asked, all innocence, and hoped that no one had told Jordan it was a tradition to end the Thursday rehearsals with pie and coffee at the drugstore's soda fountain. With luck he would leave before anyone mentioned it.

"Why, the kiss, of course," Melissa said, rolling her eyes. "Every woman in the audience will envy you. I know I do."

"I'll trade places anytime you like."

Melissa laughed. "You don't mean that. I think he's gorgeous!"

Carley glanced over at Jordan and saw Bob pointing him in the direction of the drugstore. So much for Jordan not knowing about their weekly get-together.

"I hear he grew up here," Melissa continued. "Did you know him?"

"We were in the same graduating class." Carley wasn't about to say how well she had known him. "Stacy isn't here tonight?" she asked, though she knew quite well she wasn't. Carley had to turn the subject away from Jordan.

"One of her kids is sick. There's no reason for her to come to all the rehearsals. Until we start using props, there really isn't anything for her to do. Chester gives the cues. He knows it by heart."

"Well, after all, he wrote it."

Melissa looked over at the small man. "Who would have guessed Chester would know so much about love?"

"People are fooled by appearances all the time," Carley said, shooting a glare at Jordan. He looked like any woman's dream prince, but she knew him to be a toad in disguise.

Melissa followed Carley's glance. "I wonder if Jordan will come to the drugstore."

"I have no idea."

"Don't you like him?"

"Not especially," Carley snapped.

"I thought maybe you did. I saw the way you looked at each other when you sang the duet, and it seemed to me—"

"I was just concentrating on the music."

"If I were singing a love song with him, I don't think I could concentrate on anything."

"Are you going to the drugstore?"

"Sure. It always takes me a while to unwind after rehearsals or performances."

Carley led the way out of the building, and the sultry night closed around them. "Do you think it will ever rain again?" She lifted her face to the darkness. "There isn't a breeze blowing. Not at all."

"The weatherman says this is the worst drought since the Dust Bowl of the thirties."

They crossed the empty main street and walked down the short walk to Rainwater's drugstore. Inside several of the actors sat on counter stools or in one of the four booths. Someone had put a quarter in the jukebox, and a song popular from the late sixties was playing.

"Hi, Joe," Carley said to the owner as she and Melissa slid into the second booth. "We'd like some coffee when you have time."

Joe waved his acknowledgment as he pulled a pie from the refrigerated display.

"How do you think the play will do?" Carley asked. All her senses were tuned to the door behind her, and she both hoped and feared that Jordan would come in.

"It's too soon to tell. We have a strong cast and a good director. I expect it will be one of our most successful ones."

"Mind if I sit here?" a deep voice asked.

Carley looked up to see Jordan, and her stomach did a flip-flop.

When she hesitated, he added, "I wouldn't bother you, but all the other seats are taken."

A quick glance told Carley it was true, but she couldn't possibly scoot over and let him sit beside her. The booths were so narrow that she wouldn't be able to avoid contact with him. To her chagrin, Melissa obligingly slid over, and Jordan eased in beside her. At once

Carley realized her mistake. She would have been better off occasionally bumping elbows with him than having to gaze into his mesmerizing eyes. "I really ought to get home," she murmured.

"Your coffee isn't here yet," Melissa objected. "Besides, you can sleep late tomorrow."

"Don't rush off on my account," Jordan added with a look that encouraged her to do just that.

"Are you getting settled in?" Melissa asked. "Moving can be such a pain."

"It's as if I'd never been away," he said with a smile that would make any woman feel special. With a glance at Carley he added, "In some ways."

"Carley said you were in school together," Melissa put in.

"Did she, now?" Jordan's eyes held taunting amusement.

"And that's all I told her." Carley's throat felt tight with suppressed emotion.

"Are you married, Jordan?" Melissa asked.

"Divorced."

Melissa's pink lips curved up. "So am I. At least I'm in the process of getting a divorce. As a matter of fact, I have an appointment with you next Tuesday."

"Oh?"

"Your aunt was my attorney. She was such a love. I remember..."

Carley pretended to be listening, but she found her thoughts returning to Jordan as if he were a lodestone. Why did he still affect her so strongly? When he smiled at Melissa, Carley felt a possessive jab of jealousy, yet she didn't want him. She didn't care anything about him at all. Melissa was her friend and had had a rough time in her marriage. Maybe that was it, Carley decided.

Jordan might scar Melissa even more deeply than her abusive marriage. Certainly Carley carried enough invisible scars from loving him.

She dared to look at him for a second, and, as if he were as keenly aware of her as she was of him, their eyes met.

Jordan's eyes were the color of quicksilver with dark rims and thick black lashes, and he had a way of looking at a person as though he could see into her soul. In a courtroom, Carley thought, he would be invincible. He certainly was in a soda fountain booth. She had never seen Melissa try so hard to flirt with anyone.

"I'm surprised to find the soda fountain is still here. 'Progress' has gobbled up most of them." He looked straight at Carley.

"It was. Gobbled up, I mean," Melissa said. "After we got our Main Street designation, Mr. Raintree reinstalled it. He never tries out for plays, but he's a strong supporter of our theater. He stays open late on Thursdays so we can come here to unwind."

Still looking at Carley, Jordan said, "Do you always unwind here?"

For some reason Carley felt a blush color her cheeks.

"I remember years ago that this was the gathering place. Right, Carley?"

Unbidden, the memories flooded back. She was a teenager again, with a ponytail and an armload of books, and he was the captain of the football team. And the second booth from the door had been "theirs."

Carley's blush deepened. "When we got here, the other booths were already taken."

Melissa looked confused, but Jordan smiled as if he didn't believe it for a minute.

Someone fed another nickel into the old-fashioned jukebox, and as the colors in its panels changed from yellow to orange to red to purple, the record began to play. Strains of *Summer Wine* filled the room.

Carley had heard that song dozens of times since Joe Raintree had installed the jukebox, but it had been many years since she had heard it while sitting in the second booth from the door and looking straight at Jordan Landry. Again memories overwhelmed her, memories of wearing Jordan's high school letter jacket that was so big on her it covered her hips and swallowed her arms as they danced, barely moving, to *Summer Wine*. It had been their song. And the words had been prophetically true. After Jordan left her, she had almost worn out the grooves on her copy of the song as she probed the agony of her loss. He had indeed left her craving more summer wine.

Against her will, her eyes met his, and time became frozen. All the externals fell away, leaving only Carley and Jordan and the bittersweet memories.

Why, her eyes asked silently.

I had no choice, his replied.

I loved you, her soul protested.

I loved you, his soul answered.

Carley abruptly slid out of the booth. "I have to go. No, Melissa, I really do." Again her haunted eyes met Jordan's, then she turned and walked briskly out of the drugstore.

Tears blurred her vision as she drove the few blocks to her house. She felt tense and overwrought as she fought against her need to sob aloud. "I can't do it!" she ground out as she pounded the heel of her hand against the steering wheel. "I can't go through with this!"

She braked to a stop in her drive and hurried into her house, tossing her purse on a chair. She flopped onto the couch, kicked off her shoes and stretched her legs as the sobs overtook her.

Jordan couldn't have picked a worse time to return to Apple Tree. Edward was dead and she was too lonely to be firm in her resolve to continue her animosity toward Jordan. She might have been able to cope if he had had the decency to stick to his law practice and stay out of her world. She couldn't play opposite him as a lover, practice several nights a week and kiss him in front of the entire town. Had he no sensibilities at all?

She groaned and lay back on the couch, draping her legs over the arm. Even an insensitive clod should be able to see what a miserable position this put her in! The undeniable truth must be that Jordan had so completely buried any love he had had for her that he no longer felt connected to her in any way.

Tears ran over her temples and into her hair as Carley hugged a throw pillow tightly against her breasts. She had loved Jordan with the single-minded devotion of a teenager. He had been her first love, and she had never entirely forgotten him. Perhaps no woman ever completely forgot that first sweet love, the first boy to stir her to a woman's desires, the first lips to bridge her from childhood to adulthood.

Carley thought she had shelved all she had felt for Jordan. He had married Cindy Lou for the most unromantic of reasons—pregnancy. Carley had grown to know Edward, they'd fallen in love and she had married him. True, her infatuation for Edward had been a rebound from Jordan's betrayal, but it had blossomed into a deep and caring love. Perhaps Edward had lacked the passion of a younger man, but he had provided much more emotional security. They had been friends as well as husband and wife. She had always known Edward was likely to die before she did, but she hadn't expected it to be so soon or so unexpectedly.

She blamed her loneliness for the mess her emotions were in. If Edward were still alive, she could face Jordan at any time and perform opposite him as effortlessly as if he were a stranger. It was that damned loneliness that was to blame. Because of it she was reading too much into a passing glance, the meaning of a phrase, the playing of an old song.

"Edward, why did you have to die?" she asked the empty room as she had so often when widowhood was still new and raw. And as before, there was only silence.

Jordan let himself into the house that had been his aunt's, but now was his. Tonight the house held no peace for him.

He had left the drugstore soon after Carley; all the others there were strangers, or at least that's what he told himself. He had never found any difficulty in talking to people or in making new friends, but he had seen and correctly interpreted the glint in Melissa's eyes. He would welcome her as a friend or a client but not as anything more. Melissa had a frail, victimlike quality that reminded him too much of Cindy. Melissa was interested in more than a platonic relationship. Jordan would bet anything on that. Not that he thought he was God's gift to women, but he knew pickings were slim in a small town. Any bachelor with a means of supporting himself was fair game.

He unbuttoned his shirt as he went up the stairs. The house was so big and empty. After years of small apartments he felt almost... Was there a term for something that meant the opposite of claustrophobia? Jordan had never heard the name for it if such a phobia existed.

Going into the bathroom, he shucked off his clothes and tossed them into the hamper. His aunt had not installed central air conditioning, and the bedroom window unit barely cooled the bathroom. The air was hot and close, the way he remembered it feeling when he was a boy. He turned on the tap and sluiced cold water over his face and torso. That made him feel cleaner and cooler, if not any happier.

As he dried himself, he wondered why he had really come back to Apple Tree. He no longer had family here, and the law business in Apple Tree wasn't all that challenging. Certainly not after the work he had done in Houston. And the house? It was pretty and it held fond memories, but it was only a house.

Memories. He walked naked back to the bedroom. His memories of Apple Tree weren't old friends, they were specters. They were goblins that snapped at his heels every time he saw Carley McKay.

He pulled back the covers and lay on the sheets to cool off. Within minutes his skin had cooled, but not his thoughts. What had he expected to find? Carley waiting for him in her cheerleader suit and ponytail? Carley happily married and blurred into a frumpy matron who canned tomatoes and wiped kids' runny noses? Since he'd seen her, the idea of Carley as a wife and mother was hardly that. If his life had gone right, he would be the one bringing tomatoes home to her and would have been the father of her kids.

Jordan closed his eyes and rubbed his eyelids tiredly. He didn't want to put himself back into that bracket of misery. Marriage might be fine for some, but not for him. He simply wasn't cut out for it. No matter how hard he had tried, he had not been able to make Cindy happy. Kevin had been happy, but Jordan refused to think about that. Kevin's loss still hurt too much when it was late at night and no one was around.

Instead he conjured up the memory of Edward McKay. What in the hell had Carley seen in him? True Edward had been nice-looking with this thick silver hair and Nordic blue eyes, but he was a couple of years older than Carley's father. Edward's son was older than Carley! Jordan had no problem understanding why Edward would want a beautiful young bride, but why had Carley agreed? For his money? Jordan didn't really believe that, though he would have liked to. Carley wasn't that kind of woman. They had had no children. Did that mean they hadn't . . .

Jordan growled up at the ceiling. Of course they had! Any man who had Carley in his bed would consummate the marriage. The idea twisted in his gut. Jordan felt ill at the thought of Edward McKay's hands on Carley's body. Of her giving herself to him willingly, even eagerly.

With a groan Jordan got up and pulled on a pair of shorts. Carley's private life was none of his business. Whether she had been happy wasn't his affair. He had forfeited all claim to her the night he had guzzled a six-pack of beer and let Cindy Lou Wallace seduce him in the back seat of his car behind the football stadium. Jordan had regretted that night so often that he had long since forgotten any physical pleasure he had experienced. The consequences had by far overshadowed the sensual gratification.

He went out onto the small porch that looked over the private lake. In the distance he heard a dog barking, but he knew he was far enough removed from his neighbors that he couldn't be seen. A pale half-moon was reflected as a wavering shaft of silver on the water. The trees were still and limp in the oppressive heat that lingered long into the night. In a matter of minutes his bare skin was covered with a sheen of moisture. Jordan rested his hip against the wooden railing as he looked into the night.

He should never have come back here. Apple Tree belonged to the ghosts of his past. No one could really go home again because "home" was too elusive, especially in a town like Apple Tree, where the physical aspects were tauntingly unchanged but where all the lives were altered. Time passed slowly here, but it did indeed pass.

What was Carley doing now? She had been in a hurry to leave. Maybe she had a late date with someone. Jordan frowned. He shouldn't care whether she had. Carley was free to do as she pleased.

But the night seemed even lonelier with the thought of Carley laughing with some other man. Jordan knew he should admit his mistake in returning, pack up his belongings and go, but there was his commitment to *Moonbeams and Roses*. He would finish what he had started. He wouldn't give Carley the satisfaction of driving him out of the play. With grim determination, Jordan went back into the empty house.

Chapter Four

"We made a mistake in renovating the building before we raised all the money we needed for technical equipment," Chester said for the third time. "I tried to tell you that, and no one would listen."

"Carley has the floor," the president, Ken Boudreaux, said. "Carley?"

"Admittedly it was a mistake to spend the money first on the part of the theater everyone sees, but we all thought the other pledges would come in."

"I didn't," Chester muttered. "I told you so."

"But we have to go on from here," Carley continued. "We just have to—" Carley stopped in midsentence when the door at the rear of the auditorium opened and Jordan Landry sauntered in. Everyone turned to see what had distracted her, and Jordan smiled at the gathering and nodded to them as he took a seat. Did he have to arrive late to everything? Carley thought peevishly, then she silently questioned the reasonableness of her reaction to his presence. Quickly she decided it was nothing more than just her nerves, and resumed the point she had been trying to make. "As I was saying, we just have to dig in and raise some more money."

Jordan raised his hand and was recognized by the chair. "How much is needed and for what purpose?"

Ken consulted his notes. "I don't have the exact figures with me, but we need several thousand to purchase state-of-the-art lighting equipment. Most of the lights we're using now were bought secondhand from other theaters. Some of them are quite old and the wiring in them is questionable. However, our biggest expense will be for a solid-state lighting control board."

Melissa raised her hand. "Maybe we should apply for another grant."

"That takes too long," Ken said. "I doubt our light board will make it through the run of this play."

"I was in a theater in Houston," Jordan put in. "We had some luck with fund-raising. What about a walkathon where the businesses in town pledge a certain amount for each mile walked?"

"We haven't tried that," Melissa admitted.

"Or how about a white elephant auction? Those are fun, and people will bid on the strangest things when they know the money's going for a good cause."

"This isn't Houston," Carley said coolly. "Watching somebody walk ten miles isn't our idea of a thrill. And most of our 'white elephants' are family heirlooms." She and Jordan exchanged a glare.

"Well," Melissa said hopefully, "his ideas might work."

"I think both ideas are good," Stacy added.

"Maybe a bake sale," suggested Carley.

"Cakes don't bring in much money," Jordan stated. "We could probably make that much by simply passing a hat to everybody here."

Carley knew he was right, but nevertheless she frostily replied, "We did quite well with the others. Naturally that would be a rather homespun event for Houston, but we aren't in Houston, now are we?"

Stacy looked at Carley as if Carley's face had just turned blue. She leaned toward her friend and whispered, "What's the matter with you?"

"What's he doing here?" Carley hissed back.

"It's an open meeting, for pete's sake." Stacy stared at Carley as if she couldn't believe Carley was acting this way.

Carley knew she was being snippy, but she couldn't help it. Following rehearsal the evening before, she had wondered if Jordan had gone home with Melissa. Now she was sure. When Jordan had come in, he had taken the seat next to Melissa and had obviously learned about the meeting from her.

"Who is in charge of fund-raising?" Jordan asked. "I think whoever it is should have a say in this."

"I am," Melissa said, her voice soft and low. "I think those are good ideas."

Carley frowned. Naturally Melissa would think that. As far as she was concerned, Jordan was a knight in shining armor.

"I think a walkathon is an excellent way to give people a heat stroke," Carley said.

"Then we could do it in the high school gym," Melissa suggested. "It's air conditioned, and no one is using it this summer."

"We could hold the auction here," Stacy added. "I have some things in my attic that would be perfect."

Chester spoke up. "My sister and I have a darling old lamp with gold fringe on the shade. It's so ugly it's cute."

"That's the kind of thing we need," Jordan said, leaning forward with interest. "The uglier the better."

"Wait a minute. We're already planning an auction. The annual charity benefit auction will be in our theater this year. Remember? I don't think two auctions would be a good idea," Carley protested.

"Then why don't you combine the two?" Jordan suggested.

"I like that," Ken said. "I like that a lot. We weren't expecting our share of the benefit's proceeds to be enough for what we need, but since we're sponsoring it this year, maybe the committee will agree to a change from the way its been done before. This white elephant thing sounds like a lot of fun."

"Farley Harrison is our auctioneer this year. I'll bet he won't mind. After all, how much difference can there be between selling cows in a ring and white elephants," Stacy said with a laugh.

"This sounds great," Melissa said. "If we could keep the proceeds from the sale of the extra items, we might just make enough on this and not have to have a walk-athon. But I'm going to need some help. Jordan, will you work with me to put all this together?"

"I'd be glad to."

Carley was doing a slow boil. Jordan hadn't been here a month and he was taking over the town.

"Carley, if you feel the need to bake a cake," he said in a teasing voice, "bake it with blue food coloring, and it will fit right in."

"I think I can restrain myself." She threw him a withering look, but he had turned his attention back to Melissa.

"What's wrong with you?" Stacy asked Carley again in a low voice no one else could hear. "You aren't acting at all like yourself."

Carley shook her head. She was already feeling ashamed of her cutting words. "It's just that Jordan Landry affects me like fingernails on a chalkboard."

"Evidently!"

"I'm sorry. I shouldn't have been so obvious about it."

Ken assigned Melissa the responsibility of implementing the new fund-raising plans and moved on to the next item on the agenda.

From Jordan's vantage point a row behind Carley and to one side, he watched Carley, thankful he could do so without being obvious. She sounded as if she actually hated him, and he knew she had ample reason. Still, he hoped he was wrong.

After the next Thursday rehearsal, Jordan decided against going to the drugstore with the cast. Not only did he not want to encourage Melissa, but he wanted to avoid Carley, as well. Halfway to his house he remembered that he had left his script backstage on the piano. Bob had told them to have their lines memorized by the following week, so Jordan circled a block and went back to the theater.

He had expected to have to go to the drugstore to get a key from Bob, but to his surprise the theater door was unlocked.

The stage was still lighted, and when he heard a movement behind the backdrop, he stopped. Before he could call out, he saw a woman with distinctive auburn hair come out onto the stage. By the way Carley moved he could tell she thought she was alone. For a few moments he watched as she opened a can of paint and took a paintbrush out of the back pocket of her tight-fitting faded jeans. She was wearing an old T-shirt with a Cancun logo on the front, and her hair was pulled back in the ponytail he remembered so well.

"Hello," he called out.

Carley jumped and spun about, staring blindly at the darkened auditorium. "Who's there?" she demanded nervously.

"It's me." As he moved toward the stage, he saw recognition on her face. "Why are you still here?"

"I didn't want to go to get coffee tonight."

"Neither did I."

They gazed at each other, and Jordan was forcibly struck with how much he wanted this woman. He had always wanted the unattainable. "What are you doing?"

"I'm going to start painting the flats."

"At this time of night?"

"Why not? I don't have anyone waiting up for me." Instantly her face showed her regret at having said what she did. "What are you doing here?"

"I forgot my script. If we're to be off-book by next week, I'll need to study over the weekend."

Carley pointed to the floor. "I have mine here. I plan to paint and memorize at the same time."

Jordan came up the steps and onto the stage, his thumbs hooked in the pockets of his jeans. "You shouldn't be here all alone so late at night."

She looked away as she shrugged. "There's nothing here at night that isn't here in the daytime."

"I can't imagine any woman working late at night in Houston without locking the door. Are you expecting someone?"

"No, and this isn't Houston."

He sauntered nearer and looked down at the opened can of paint. "Blue?"

"It's been approved by the board," she said defensively.

Jordan squatted down beside her as she sat on the floor. "I wasn't complaining. I think it will look good."

"There's a script back there on the piano that is probably yours. Don't let me detain you."

"You aren't." He watched as she began applying the paint to the canvas flat. She looked so young in her jeans and T-shirt and with her hair pulled back that way. We could almost pretend that no time had passed since they were sweethearts.

"It's hard to believe you were married to Edward McKay," he said absently.

"Are you going to start in on that again?" She stopped painting to glare up at him. "I would rather not discuss it, if you don't mind."

"What would you prefer to talk about?"

"I would prefer that you just leave and go home."

"I don't think I should do that. You may feel safe doing this, but I disagree. If I could wander in, so could anyone else."

"Nonsense. I often work here at night, sometimes very late, and I've never seen anyone at all."

"Why do you work at night?"

Carley frowned. She didn't want to admit she did it out of loneliness. "It's always quiet then. During the day the janitor and the manager are in and out. At night I can be alone."

"Why do you do it at all?"

"Because I'm in charge of set design," she said in exasperation. "This is a small theater, and it takes a lot of work from everyone. Most of us have at least two significant responsibilities. I'm on set design and the play-reading committee."

"Both of those sound interesting. Is there an opening for me on those committees?"

Carley's pulse began to race as her ambivalent feelings again went to war. She was forced to remain silent to control her emotions. Finally she said, "What exactly do you want from me?"

"Want from you? Nothing."

She studied his eyes. He looked as if he were telling the truth. "Then why do you want to be on my committees?"

"As I said, both of those jobs interest me. I did some set design work with my theater group in Houston, and I have seen a lot of plays."

"Plays that do well in a city aren't necessarily good in Apple Tree. You'd be surprised at what people have objected to."

"You can't please everybody all the time."

"So we've learned. I doubt there has ever been anything written that someone couldn't find objectionable in some way or another."

"City dwellers tend to be more liberal minded about their entertainment," he agreed. "You missed a spot there."

Carley brushed paint over the place Jordan indicated. "This is the first civil conversation we've had."

"It's the first one since my return, yes."

Carley frowned. "That's obviously what I meant."

"Is there another paintbrush? I can help. I'm not in any rush to go home."

"You'll get paint all over your good clothes. I keep these old ones here at the theater just to paint in."

"Maybe I could help some other way. How about if I change around the flats so the doors and windows are in the right places?"

"I can do that later." She had intended to do that before she started painting, but his presence had rattled her.

"That's a two-person job."

"I've done it alone before."

The diagram of the set design Carley had worked out with Bob Horton was on the seat of a nearby chair. Jordan picked it up and studied it. "We need to swap places with the back door and that window. Is there a flat with an arched doorway?"

"It's stored in the back room." Carley stood and laid her wet brush on the top of the paint can. "We never struck the set from the last play. We often use the same flats each time, but of course in a different arrangement."

"I'll get the archway."

Carley went behind the flat and pulled the pins that held the standard doorframe in place. Gradually she eased the door, frame and all, out of the opening. After leaning it against the back wall out of the way, she untied the cotton rope that lashed the flats together. Although the flat was awkward due to its size, it was no heavier than a painting that size would be.

She carried it stage right and was taking out a window when Jordan returned.

"Let me help you with that."

"I can manage. I do this all the time."

Jordan reached over her, and Carley found herself encircled by his arms as he caught the windowframe. For a moment neither of them moved. She was all too aware of the faint scent of his cologne and the more sensual aroma that was distinctly Jordan, one that reminded her of fresh air and sunshine. She always used to tease him that he smelled better than his cologne. She could feel the heat of his body near her back and a stirring of his breath in her hair.

"You can do it," she conceded hastily as she ducked under his arm. "Just put it over there."

Jordan paused, then lifted the window out of the opening. He was silent as he leaned it against the wall; his lips were tight.

Carley's fingers trembled as she untied the ropes that secured the window flat to the ones adjacent to it. Moving scenery had never been a sensual experience before.

Jordan put the archway in the opening where the window had been, and Carley expertly lashed it in place. He studied it a minute and said, "Let's put that extra door flat behind the arch to give the illusion of another room."

"I had planned to use a plain one there."

"But if we use a closed door and put it off center, it will look as if there really is a house back there. It will give the set more depth."

"Did you come back to town with the intention of changing everything, or did you decide to do it just to irritate me?"

"You're pretty easily irritated," he observed. "One of my uncles used to have a theory about that. It had to do with a person's sex life—or rather lack of it."

Carley blazed bright red. "Your Uncle Ned is full of it!"

Jordan grinned. "That's the uncle I had in mind, all right." More seriously he asked, "Is Uncle Ned right?"

"Mind your own business." She picked up the window and startled to lug it toward the side of the stage.

"Quit carrying things that are too heavy for you." He took the window away from her and carried it effortlessly to the proper spot.

Carley lifted the flat and put it into position with more zeal than was necessary. Jordan's question about her sex life was still rankling her. "Melissa said you gave her a ride to rehearsal tonight."

"That's right. Her car is in the shop. Tracy volunteered to take her home."

"I like Melissa."

"So do I." He fitted the window back into the opening, and Carley turned the thumb latches on the back side to lock it in place.

"I wouldn't want her to get hurt."

"What's that supposed to mean?" He rested his palms on the windowsill and gazed through it at her.

"Melissa is coming out of a very distasteful situation."

"Yes, I know. I'm representing her."

As if he hadn't spoken, Carley continued, "She was mentally and physically abused for years."

"Her husband is nothing but trash. I have a low opinion of any man who would abuse a woman."

"So do I. That's why I feel so protective of her. Melissa has been through enough misery."

"Meaning?"

"She isn't thinking clearly enough at the moment to tell what may or may not be best for her."

"I know you're aiming at something. Get to the point."

"I don't want you to hurt her."

"Me! I've never hit a woman in my entire life!"

"I didn't mean that. I was referring to Melissa's feelings. She will be badly hurt if you string her along and then drop her."

Jordan glared at her as if he couldn't believe what he was hearing. "I have no intention of hurting her, Carley!"

"No? I know for a fact that you're capable of it." She felt a waspish urge to wound him. She wanted him to feel just a sampling of the emotional hurt he had inflicted so thoughtlessly on her.

For a long while he was silent, and Carley wondered if she had gone too far. When he spoke, his voice was tightly controlled. "I won't hurt Melissa. As a matter of fact, I feel protective toward her, just as you do."

Pain squeezed Carley's heart. "I see." She thought of Melissa's wistful mannerisms and her delicate bone structure, her large blue eyes and moonbeam-pale hair. Melissa was the sort to inspire protectiveness in a man. She had an air of helplessness that suddenly reminded Carley of Cindy Lou. Melissa was just his type. She turned abruptly and yanked the rope taut.

"I was trying to reassure you," Jordan said in a tense voice. "Why are you getting angry?"

"I'm not angry!" She dragged the door and frame down stage. Jordan didn't move to help her. "Well? Aren't you going to do your part?"

"I thought you didn't need any help."

"Put your foot against the flat to brace it."

"Here." He came to aid her. "Let me lift it in and you brace it."

Carley quickly dodged around to the front before she found herself surrounded by his arms again. "I guess we can try the closed door behind the archway and see how it looks. We can always move it again."

"You've become rather opinionated over the years," he observed. "I don't recall you being stubborn just for the sake of stubbornness."

"I'm not stubborn at all. It's just that you aren't automatically right about everything."

She stepped back to critically view the set and to compare it with her diagram. "That looks good." As he went to the back room to get the door and flat to make a hallway, she resumed painting.

"There!" After Jordan had put the extra door in place, he went out into the auditorium and studied the set. "Much better."

Carley gave him a dirty look.

"Where's a paint roller?" he asked as he came back on stage.

"I prefer to use a brush." She was trying hard not to lose her temper, but it was fraying at the edges.

"But you can put on a thinner layer with a roller. I've always—"

"Jordan, just get out of here and leave me alone!"

"No way, lady. My guess is that you're here because your house is lonely and the nights are too long."

"You presume a hell of a lot!"

"I don't hear you denying it."

"That's because I have too much class to discuss my love life with you!" She glared at him as if she was considering hitting him with the paint brush.

"I've been back in town for weeks. If you had a love life, someone would have told me by now. Bob says you don't date at all."

"He did what? I can't believe you had the nerve to ask him something like that!"

"I didn't. He volunteered it. I think he planned to do some matchmaking between us."

"What! Just wait until I see him again!"

"I've already told him to lay off."

Carley felt as if the wind were punched out of her sails. She might not want to date Jordan again, but she was wounded that he felt the same way and that he had said as much to Bob Holton. "Good!" she bluffed.

"I didn't tell him about . . . that we had once gone together."

"It was a lot more serious than that," she snapped. "I seem to recall we were engaged!"

"I saw no reason to tell Bob that. You can if you want to."

Tears stung Carley's eyes, and she turned back to her painting. "I'm doing my best to forget that. So should you."

"That's not so simple when you always make such a point of reminding me."

"That does it!" Carley grabbed the can of paint and stalked backstage.

"Where are you going?"

"To wash out my paintbrush!" She blinked hard to keep her brimming tears from rolling down her cheeks. No one in the entire world could infuriate her to the extent Jordan Landry did. Even the sound of his voice was like sandpaper on her nerves.

She hammered the lid back on the paint can and went into the small bathroom used by the actors. She turned on the water in the sink and scrubbed angrily at the paintbrush. She was so upset, she knew she wouldn't sleep a wink all night.

"What are you so angry about?" His deep voice seemed to fill the tiny room.

Carley jumped. "I thought you left." He was standing in the doorway behind her.

"Why are you so angry?" he repeated.

"Because of you," she stormed. "You make me angry. Everything about you makes me furious! The sound of your voice, the way you move, the smell of your skin..." She faltered. "Everything!"

"Why do you suppose that is?" His voice was mellow and rich.

"I suppose because you jilted me to marry a bimbo!"

"Cindy isn't a bimbo!"

"No? You couldn't prove it by what happened, could you? And why isn't there a name for a male bimbo!"

"The term doesn't apply to me, either!"

"You think not? You're the one Cindy Lou named as the father of her child. You didn't even try to deny it!"

He glared down at her as if he, too, were losing his temper.

"See? You still don't!"

"You and I had argued, and we'd broken up! At least I thought we had!"

"Oh, sure! Funny that I don't remember that." She glared at him scornfully.

"Then you have a faulty memory, because that's exactly what happened!"

"I don't remember—"

"It was the weekend after the prom. You got mad because I insisted on going to college at the University of Texas, and you wanted us both to go to Stephen F. Austin!"

"I never—" Carley broke off. She did recall something about that. "But we never split up. I would have remembered that!"

"We did for that weekend. You said you never wanted to see me again."

Carley frowned and snapped her mouth shut. That seemed familiar, too.

"So I went out with Cindy and a six-pack of beer. By Monday you called and we made up, but by then the damage was done."

Carley shut off the water so hard that the pipes vibrated in the wall. "I don't want to talk about it."

"That's a typical female answer," he scoffed.

She wheeled on him. "Whatever the reason, Cindy Lou got pregnant and you got married!"

"So did you!" He matched her glare for glare. "While we're casting stones, maybe you'd better examine your own history. I married Cindy because I had to or lose my self-respect. Why did you marry McKay?"

"I loved him!"

"Come on, Carley! An old man like that? How could you ever get to know him well enough to know that? You didn't exactly travel in the same social circles, for God's sake! I can't imagine a man in McKay's position in this town coming on to a girl fresh out of high school. You had to have been the one to initiate it!"

All the blood drained from Carley's face. She threw the brush in the sink, leaving a spray of water on the counter backsplash and pushed him aside as she hurried from the room. As she passed the dressing room, she grabbed up her clean clothes.

"Carley, wait!"

She didn't pause. She crossed the stage, snatched up her script and flipped the breaker, plunging the set into darkness. Behind her she heard Jordan curse as he tripped over a prop box.

Carley made her way toward the lobby with the aid of the dim aisle safety lights. Usually she felt uneasy after the theater lights were off, but tonight she was too angry.

She heard Jordan stumble onto the stage, but she didn't look back. He could find his way out. After all, he had said he knew all about theaters.

She brushed past the curtains that separated the well-lit lobby from the auditorium. For security reasons these lights and those out front stayed on all night. As she went outside, she flipped the latch on the door lock. When Jordan closed the door behind him, it would automatically lock.

"Damn it, Carley, wait a minute!"

She heard him call to her, but she only quickened her pace. By the time Jordan reached the sidewalk, she was driving away from the curb. She wiped angrily at the tears that coursed down her cheeks. Edward really had been the one to pursue her, but when Jordan said it, it sounded so . . . lecherous. Edward hadn't been that way at all! He had been good and kind! Jordan had no right to tarnish her memory of Edward! Carley wished Jordan Landry had never come back to town.

Chapter Five

"If I didn't love you, would I have asked you to marry me? Would I want you to have my children?" Jordan glared down at Carley, his words clipped.

"I want to have your children, but I also want a career." Carley's fist was balled on her hip, and anger smoldered in her dark eyes.

"Wait a minute, wait a minute," Bob interrupted as he waved them to silence. He frowned down at his script. "Something is wrong here."

"I know *my* lines," Carley said with a toss of her head at Jordan.

"I know mine, too," he retorted.

"Yeah, the lines are right." Bob perused the script again.

Chester bounced from his seat. "It's wrong, I tell you. It's all wrong. They're doing it *wrong*."

Bob ran his finger down the page, trying to ignore Chester. "Buck, let's go back to the part where you propose to Alice. Start with, 'Listen to that mockingbird.'"

Jordan moved back up and stage left and resumed his stony stare out the fake window. "'Listen to that mockingbird, Alice. Spring is here. They're making a nest.'"

Carley stalked over to stand beside him. From her expression, one could only assume she was planning to make mockingbird stew. "'They must be in love.'"

"'Yeah, like we are.'" Jordan glared down at her. "'I feel just like that mockingbird.'"

"'Oh?'" Her tone implied he was about as smart as the bird as well.

"'I want to make a nest for you. To take care of you.'" His tone held a clear threat.

"'I'd like to take care of you, too, Buck,'" she growled.

"No, no," Chester wailed. "That's all wrong."

Bob frowned up at his two stars. "Do you two feel okay?"

"I feel perfectly fine," Carley said. "I had a very restful weekend."

"I'll bet you did," Jordan said with acid politeness.

She glared at him. "Not *that* restful."

"Okay," Bob said in confusion. "What seems to be wrong up there?"

"There's nothing wrong with me," Jordan said with a scowl at Carley.

"No problem here, Bob," she said. "At least not with me."

Bob pursed his lips and shook his head. "Maybe it's me. Okay, let's try it again."

"'I want to make a nest for you,'" Jordan said as he glared at the window. "'To take of care you.'"

"'I'd like to take care of you, too, Buck. Permanently.'" She made a parody of a smile.

"'You're reminding me more and more of that damned bird,'" Jordan said.

"No, no, no!" Chester said as he paced and wrung his hands. "Those aren't the right lines."

"*Line*," Jordan barked toward Stacy, who was serving as prompter.

"The line is 'Your skin is as soft as a bird's feathers; your voice is as sweet as its song.'" Stacy stared across the stage. "I said—"

"I got it." Jordan drew a deep breath and said with no conviction at all, "'Your skin is as soft as a bird's feathers; your voice is as sweet as its song.'" He made it sound more like an insult than a compliment.

"Thanks a lot!"

"Give her the line, Stacy," Bob called.

"Never mind, I remember." Carley jerked her chin up at Jordan. "'I wish life was as uncomplicated for me as it is for that bird.'"

"'Marry me, Alice. I'll make you think uncomplicated.'"

Chester whined as if he were in pain and sank into a seat.

"Hold on, you two." Bob tossed his script onto the seat beside him and stood up. "Carley, can I talk to you for a minute?"

She left the stage and fell into step beside Bob as he strolled up the aisle. He companionably looped his arm around her shoulders. "What's the trouble?" he asked as if he were her big brother.

"Nothing. I just had a rough weekend, that's all."

"No, don't give me that. I know you better than that. What's wrong? Is it the way it's written?"

Carley sighed. She couldn't blame Chester for her trouble. "No, it's not that."

"Are you having trouble memorizing this much?" he asked in genuine concern for her. "You've never had the lead role before."

"No! I mean, I know my lines. It's Jordan. I . . . I'm having trouble playing opposite him."

"Ahh," he said as if he were trying to understand but had no clue what she was talking about.

"He gives me the wrong cue and it throws me off. Besides, I just plain don't like him."

"So the problem is Jordan, huh?"

Carley felt guilty, but she nodded.

"Now I understand. I'll have a talk with him and straighten him out. Okay?"

She smiled timorously. "Thanks, Bob. And I appreciate you not making me complain about him in front of everyone."

"Do I look like Attila the Hun?" He hugged her with a bone-crushing squeeze. "Okay now?"

"I'm fine."

They walked back down to the stage as Bob explained exactly how he wanted her to play the scene. "Jordan? Can I talk to you for a minute?" he said as Carley resumed her place on stage.

When he and Jordan were out of earshot from the others, Bob said, "I've had a talk with Carley, and I think I have her straightened out now."

"I hope you weren't rough on her," Jordan said in a low voice.

"No, no. Carley and I are old friends."

Jordan frowned. He had seen Bob's arm across her shoulders and had observed the hug. "I threw her off, I guess."

"I see."

"I had a hard weekend."

"Oh?"

"I had a lot on my mind. Couldn't seem to concentrate."

"I guess having to act opposite Carley is a problem for you, from all I've heard around town."

"You can say that again."

"Well, don't let it get you down. Okay?" He slapped Jordan on the back as if they were the best of friends. "Hang in there."

"Don't worry, I will."

Bob was smiling like a Cheshire cat as he resumed his seat in the fifth row. "Okay. Let's do it again."

This time Jordan's voice was more that of a lover as he discussed the mockingbird. Carley's reply was gentle and edged with longing as if she really did wish she could say yes to the proposal.

As she gazed up into his eyes, she felt a tug on her heart. They had said these words before and had meant them. True, they had been phrased differently, but the idea had been the same. His eyes had been just as silver, his face no less earnest. And she had said yes.

"'I can't give you an answer, Buck.'" She turned away to keep her eyes from revealing her true thoughts.

"'You mean you can't give me the answer I want.'" He thought how the lights made her hair as rich and glossy as if it were spun silk. Regret for what should have been swept over him. He had slept very little since rehearsals started. His mind was too full of Carley.

She wore her hair in a different style these days and had learned to apply makeup in a way that accentuated her natural beauty, but beneath the eye shadow and mascara her eyes were still widely innocent. Her body had matured into graceful curves, and her movements were fluid and feminine. But Jordan had the distinct impression that she wasn't happy. This didn't surprise him. Carley had always hated being alone. She must be terribly lonely in that big, rambling house. Jordan was lonely in his.

He jerked away. His lines took all his concentration. Stacy fed him the cue when he faltered.

Had Chester never been in love? Jordan wondered to himself. These weren't the words a man would say to win a woman's love. If he could paraphrase them, he could tell her what was in his heart. Buck's heart, he amended hastily.

Her eyes met his, and he saw the hurt in them. Was it real or was she merely getting into Alice's skin? Tears gathered, and her voice broke slightly as she delivered her line. She was acting, he told himself. That was all. Carley was a damned good actress. He was a fool even to consider that there might be more behind her memorized words.

"I thought we would never finish tonight," Carley said as she helped Stacy arrange the props for the next rehearsal. They were alone in the dark building; everyone else had left for the soda fountain.

"Once Melissa learns her lines, it will go more smoothly."

"I've never known her to be so slow in getting off-book," Carley said as she smoothed the tablecloth over the small table.

"I guess she's distracted."

"By Jordan, you mean? All the women are except for me. Bob said Shelley has volunteered to help with makeup, and I think it's just so she can get to know him." Carley frowned at her friend. "Don't look at me that way; you know what a flirt Shelley is."

"I was wondering why you care."

"Me? I don't care at all." Carley busied herself smoothing nonexistent wrinkles from the cloth. "It's just that Shelley is married, and I don't think it's right."

"You never cared before."

"Where do I put the diary?"

"On the table by the chair."

Carley put the small book in place and said, "Is that everything?"

"Let me close the curtains first." Stacy pulled the fabric over the window and consulted her script. "That's all."

"Do you mind if we skip coffee tonight?"

"I was going to suggest the same thing. Little Billy still isn't feeling well, and Bill never knows what to do with him."

"It's not serious, is it?"

"No, just a summer cold, but he's cranky."

Carley slipped the straps of her purse over her shoulder. "I always wanted children. I even had their names picked out when I was a teenager." She laughed. "From the ones I had chosen, it's probably just as well that I never had any."

"It's still not too late to remarry and have a family."

"At thirty-three? I'm not so sure about that."

"Women are having babies later in life these days."

"Besides, there's nobody in Apple Tree that interests me."

"Nobody at all? What about your leading man?"

"Especially not him."

"What is it with you two? Did something happen the night I missed rehearsal?"

"No, it happened a long time ago." Carley turned and headed out of the building before she said too much. She waited on the sidewalk out front of the theater while Stacy secured the door, then together they walked down the block to Stacy's car. Across the street the drugstore's lights glowed like jewels in the darkness. Inside she saw Jordan leaning on the counter, talking to Melissa. All at once she needed to confide in someone. "Did you know we dated in high school?"

"You and Jordan? No, I didn't know."

"We went steady. In fact, we talked about getting married."

"Are you serious?"

"You must be the only one in town who doesn't know. My phone has been ringing constantly since the play was cast."

"So what happened?"

"He married someone else."

"Why?"

"She was pregnant."

"Oh."

"So now you know why Jordan holds no charms for me. He's completely untrustworthy."

"That was a long time ago." Stacy followed Carley's gaze toward the soda fountain. "Maybe he's changed."

"I doubt it," Carley said darkly. "I just hope he doesn't break Melissa's heart."

"It's not the sort of thing you could tell her. You know how Melissa is. She would just deny any interest in him."

"I know. Honestly, I don't see how she floats through life. I guess that's one reason she put up with Jack for so long."

"Maybe. I wouldn't have put up with him at all. What a sleazy guy!"

"She's too soft-hearted for her own good."

They got in Stacy's car, and as she drove away, she said, "If Billy's dump truck is in the way, just toss it in the backseat."

Carley held the toy and turned the rubber wheels. "I wonder why Jordan came back? Oh, I know he says it's because his aunt left him the house and all, but I wonder if that's really the reason."

"What else could it be?"

Carley looked out at the houses they passed. Windows were lit; families were inside. "I suppose there is no other reason."

"I noticed he and Melissa came to rehearsal together tonight."

"Oh?" Carley had noticed that, too, but she didn't want to admit it.

"Have you tried talking to him? Maybe you could work out your differences."

"No way. I've tried talking to him, and it just ended in an argument." Her eyes flashed with anger. "He actually accused me of marrying Edward for his money!"

"No! Why, that's ridiculous. You two were happy together. Everyone knows that."

Carley frowned out at the darkness. "We weren't wildly passionate, but he was a lot older than I was. We really were happy."

Stacy made no comment, and Carley let the silence build. Finally she said, "Jordan and I probably wouldn't have been happy together, anyway."

"Not if he was getting other girls pregnant," Stacy observed.

"You know, a lot of people questioned if it was really his child. Cindy Lou, that's her name, was sleeping with half the boys in town."

"There was some doubt, and he married her, anyway?" Stacy asked in surprise.

"Obviously there was no doubt in his mind because he married her. I'll never forget the day he told me. I thought I would die."

"That must have been horrible."

"It was. There's no way to lead up to something like that. He had to just come right out and say it."

"At least *he* told you instead of letting you hear about it from someone else."

"Yes. At least he had the decency to tell me himself." She sighed. "Anyway, now you know why it's so hard for me to even be civil to him, much less perform on stage with him."

"I can certainly see why. I'm surprised you didn't drop out of the play. You have ample reason."

"No way. I've wanted to be Alice ever since I first read this play. If anyone drops out, it will have to be Jordan. I was here first and I plan to stay."

"Do you think he may drop out? We're well into rehearsal."

"No, he's probably too stubborn. That always was a failing with him."

"I hope he doesn't. I mean, I know it's hard on you, but he's such a good actor. Not to mention how handsome he is."

"It's only skin deep," Carley said.

"Evidently."

As Stacy pulled up in Carley's drive, Carley thanked her for the ride and for being there to listen.

"Hey, what are friends for?" Stacy answered with a smile, then bade Carley good night.

As Carley crossed the drive in the beam of Stacy's headlights, she felt curiously traitorous to have talked about Jordan that way, yet everything she had said was true. Why, she wondered as she fitted her key into the lock, did she feel any responsibility toward him at all? Obviously he felt nothing whatsoever about her. Carley knew that telling Stacy was the same thing as confiding in the fencepost—it would go no further. All the same, she felt guilty. If Jordan truly had changed, she had no right telling anyone why he had left town so long ago. Even if he hadn't changed, she had no right. She had no rights in regard to him at all.

Locking the door behind her, Carley headed into the kitchen. The room was black and white and austere. Etchings of French floral prints were embossed on the white cabinet doors. The countertops looked as smooth and cool as new snow. All the appliances and the sink were gleaming black. The only splashes of color were the copper canisters, pans and the hanging pot of ferns and ivy. Carley didn't especially like to cook, and she had thought if she made the kitchen original enough she would spend more time in it. That had not been the case, however.

She poured a glass of red wine and went through the swinging door into the dining room, which had also been done in stark black and white, and on into the den. Peach, she thought as she settled onto her comfortable couch. Maybe if she painted the kitchen peach, she would go in there more often. But what was the point?

She had no family to cook for, and her maid, Abby, preferred Carley to stay out.

She sipped the wine and hoped it would relax her enough for her to sleep. In the past year she had begun to stay up later and later. Unfortunately she still awoke early every morning. She needed a hobby, she told herself. Something other than the theater. Something that Jordan Landry would have no part of. But nothing came to mind.

Jordan looked down at Melissa's blue eyes and thought how much he preferred brown ones. He had hoped Carley would come to the soda fountain tonight. Everyone had said she usually did, but since the play had started she had only been over once. He wondered why he cared. He couldn't talk to her during rehearsals because offstage conversation was too distracting to the ones who were saying their lines. She always arrived exactly on time and left before he could talk to her. For a while Jordan had wondered if she and Bob were more than friends, but Bob had said he was all but engaged to a woman in a nearby town. Jordan had no reason to suspect that Bob wasn't telling the truth.

As far as Jordan could tell, Carley wasn't seeing anyone at all. He found that remarkable. The Carley he'd known in high school wasn't cut out for the celibate life. He would have bet any amount of money on that. But maybe she had changed.

"I hope you don't mind driving me home," Melissa was saying. "My car will be out of the shop tomorrow."

"No bother at all."

"I also appreciate your taking my divorce case." She lowered her eyes in embarrassment. "It was hard to file it in the first place, and I just want it to be over and done with."

"It soon will be. I expect we'll get a court date any day now. My guess is that the divorce and the play will both come off at about the same time."

"Thank goodness I have a small part this time. Although having lines to memorize has helped keep my mind occupied, I couldn't have handled a bigger role."

"I think you're doing awfully well, all things considered."

Her voice dropped lower, and he had to lean forward to hear her. "Could we go? I need to tell you something that I don't want anyone else to hear."

"Sure." Jordan paid for their coffee and called out goodbyes to some of the other cast members.

As Jordan threaded his way through the quiet town toward Melissa's house, she sat next to him on the front seat, staring out at the unblinking moon and not speaking a word. Even though the windows were up and the air conditioning was on because of the sultry night air, Jordan knew the crickets were singing for rain in the grass beneath the elm trees. After patiently waiting as long as he could, Jordan said, "So what is it you wanted to tell me?"

Melissa turned toward Jordan as if almost startled. "It's Jack. Jack called me again today."

"Did you tell him you will have a restraining order placed on him if he doesn't leave you alone?"

"He says I'm his wife and no piece of paper can keep him away. I'm scared."

"Was he drinking?"

"He always is these days."

"Men say a lot of things they don't mean when they've had too much booze."

"He meant it. He said he's going to come after me one of these nights and teach me a lesson."

"I guess he didn't say when he plans to do this."

She shook her head, and her pale hair tumbled about her face.

Jordan thought this was probably an idle threat. If Jack really meant to harm her, he would have already done so. On the other hand, she knew Jack, and Jordan didn't. "Exactly what did he say?"

"Awful things. Mostly sexual things I can't even repeat. And he said he would fix my face so no one would ever want me again."

Jordan frowned. Melissa clearly believed the threats, and Jack had put her in the hospital before. "Do you have relatives you can stay with?"

"Yes, my mother. But she lives in Dallas, and I couldn't possibly commute to my job from there. Besides, the realtor says my house will show better and sell quicker with me living in it. And if I expect to get a good recommendation from my employer, I have to finish out the three weeks' notice I've given. I don't have a degree and I need his recommendation to get another job after I move."

"Could your mother or someone else come and stay with you?"

"No, my mother is all the family I have, and she works in Dallas. She couldn't take off for three weeks. Besides, I don't want her to know how bad it's been. She worries as it is."

Jordan pulled into her driveway and parked. The house was small but neat. Although it wasn't in the better part of town, it was in a pleasant neighborhood.

He started to suggest that she call one of her neighbors for help if Jack came around causing trouble, but thought better of it. It would be good to have a witness, but with Jack potentially violent, the risk might be too great. "You do have the phone number of the police handy, don't you?"

"Sure. But in the past, they haven't been very responsive to my calls. You know Jack used to work there, and a lot of the officers are still his friends. There's no telling what he told them about me."

"If you call them, they have to come."

"Last time it took them over an hour to get here. By then Jack had calmed down and left."

"This was after your separation?"

"Yes, about two weeks ago."

"I'll talk to the chief about it."

"I doubt it will do any good, but go ahead."

Jordan frowned. He had a feeling she was right. With so many people in town kin to one another, it probably was difficult for the officers to be sufficiently detached.

Melissa got out of the car, and Jordan walked her through the wire fence gate to her door. She unlocked it and hesitated. "I hate coming home after dark," she admitted.

"Why don't you leave a light burning?"

"It's hard enough to make ends meet without lighting an empty house."

"Would you feel better if I went in and checked it out?"

"You wouldn't mind?" she asked with obvious relief. "I felt strange asking you to do that. After all, I'm a grown woman."

Jordan smiled. "I don't mind. In fact, if it will make you feel safer, and if you want me to, I'll follow you home after all the rehearsals."

Melissa gave him her singularly sweet smile. "That's not necessary. It's just that I'm nervous tonight because of that phone call."

Jordan flipped on the light switch and went into the small kitchen. Like the outside of the house, he found the inside to be old and worn but spotlessly clean. Melissa set her purse down on the countertop in an attempt to cover a badly worn spot. He smiled to put her at her ease.

The kitchen reminded him of his mother's. The stove was white and unwieldy, as was the round-edged refrigerator. Dish towels hung from a swing-arm rack, and there were cotton curtains across the window. A table with chrome legs and a Formica top stood to one side. The linoleum floor covering was a red brick pattern.

Melissa hung behind him as he methodically checked the living room, bedroom and bath. Sensing her fear was still unabated, he also looked in the closet. "All clear," he pronounced.

"Thank you. I feel so foolish." She went to a window and raised it to let in whatever breeze might happen by. "Usually I leave the windows open, but tonight . . . The house isn't usually this hot." She went to a switch and turned on the attic exhaust fan. "Can I get you some lemonade?"

Jordan found he was no more eager to go home to loneliness than she was. "I'd like that. Thanks."

Melissa went back in the kitchen and raised the window over the sink before getting an ice tray out of the refrigerator. As she ran water over the tray, the ice crackled. With a quick jerk she pulled up the metal release, freeing the ice cubes. "The play is coming along nicely. I'll have my lines down by next Thursday."

"I had trouble concentrating tonight," he said as he watched her drop the ice cubes into two jelly glasses.

"I'm glad Carley is playing Alice. I've been hoping she would get a lead role," she said as she filled the glasses with lemonade.

Jordan said something under his breath that Melissa didn't understand. "I beg your pardon?"

"Nothing. I didn't say anything."

As nonchalantly as she could, Melissa said, "I hear you two used to date."

"That was a long time ago. We've both been married since then."

"But now you aren't." She looked across at him. "Are you seeing each other again?"

He laughed. He had forgotten how everyone in a small town minded everyone else's business. "No way."

Melissa smiled. "If you had said yes, I would have felt guilty about asking you in. Carley's my friend."

"She is?" Somehow Jordan had thought all Carley's friends belonged to the country club and drove sleek new cars.

"We met through the theater. I was so sad when her husband died. They were awfully happy together."

"They were?"

"You wouldn't have thought they would be, since he was so much older than she is, but they were. Oh, I don't mean they went everywhere together or anything like that, but they had a steady marriage. He didn't even object to her being involved in the theater."

"Why would he?"

She laughed as she put the lemonade and ice back into the refrigerator. "You know how small towns are.

It's okay for a woman in Carley's social position to attend a play, but not to be in one.''

"I thought attitudes like that went out with hoop skirts.''

"Not in Apple Tree." She sat at the table, and Jordan sat opposite her. "I wish Carley would find someone. I know I'm an incurable romantic, but that's the way I am.''

"There's nothing wrong with being a romantic." He tasted the lemonade. "This is good. I haven't had lemonade in years.''

"I drink tons of it. It's all that seems to cool me down. Mom has an air conditioner, thank goodness. I can hardly wait.''

"So you plan to live with her?''

Melissa nodded. "It makes more sense for us to pool our paychecks. At least for a while. You know, until I meet some people there and decide where I want to live.''

"I'll miss you." He smiled at her. Melissa deserved so much more than she had. He took air conditioning as much for granted as a bed to sleep in. She had had few compliments, he could tell. His saying she would be missed brought a blush to her cheeks.

"Jordan, please don't tell anyone what I said about Jack. About him threatening me, I mean. It's so embarrassing.''

"Anything you tell me will be confidential.''

"Carley and Stacy know he mistreated me, but I don't want them to know about the threats. They might feel they ought to do something about it, and that might make matters worse.''

"Maybe you could stay with one of them," he suggested.

"For three weeks? No one welcomes company for that long a visit."

"I guess not."

"Besides, it's a matter of pride. I've got to learn to stand on my own feet."

"I admire your courage." Jordan stood and put his empty glass in the sink. "Thanks for the lemonade."

"Thank you for seeing me safely inside. You're welcome here anytime," she added softly.

Jordan grinned and let himself out the door. He heard her turn the lock behind him, and his heart went out to this woman who was so afraid and with such good reason. He tapped on the pane and called out, "If you need me, just give me a call."

She hesitated, then nodded.

He walked to his car and started it up. He liked Melissa and felt she deserved better than she had gotten. Maybe in Dallas she would find a man to love who would treat her right. As he drove home he whistled a tune from *Moonbeams and Roses*.

Chapter Six

Carley dressed with care for the auction. She and Stacy had spent two days collecting and arranging items donated from all over town, ranging from a bust of Lincoln carved from a salt block to a cruise of the Bahamas. Carley hadn't been to the Bahamas in years, and she had every intention of bidding on the tickets. Each year Apple Tree had a dinner and auction to benefit a charity or a worthy cause, and every year Carley was the highest bidder on the premium item.

The gown she had chosen for the occasion floated about her slender body like a shimmer of seaweed, its pale verdant hues perfectly complementing her skin tone and vibrantly contrasting with the fiery glow of her hair. After gathering her auburn tresses up onto the top of her head so that the curls would tumble down, she secured it with pearl clips. Around her neck she fastened a necklace of pale gold pearls, which had been a birthday gift from Edward. As she fastened the matching pearls to her earlobes, Carley smiled sadly. Edward had always made such a production of her birthdays and teased her that she would soon catch up with him.

Her eyes went to a silver framed photograph taken the year before he died. He had been a handsome man. She picked up the photo and studied the familiar face. To her distress she realized she couldn't remember exactly how his cologne had smelled. She had thought she would never forget anything about him. Would she soon forget the sound of his voice? She tried harder to recall the unique fragrance, and for a minute she thought she had it, but then realized she was remembering the scent Jordan wore.

Jordan. She hoped he wouldn't be at the auction. Perhaps he wouldn't. The event was black tie, and he had always detested formal dress. But that was years ago when Jordan had even rebelled against wearing a necktie. Now he dressed in a suit and tie every day. Because Melissa hadn't asked to borrow a dress, and Carley knew she didn't own anything formal, maybe she wouldn't come. And if she didn't, Jordan probably wouldn't, either.

Carley frowned. She had begun to automatically associate Jordan with Melissa in her mind. She wanted Melissa to find someone to love, but she had not wanted Jordan to be the one.

Taking her evening bag from the bed, Carley went downstairs. "Abby?"

"Yes, ma'am?" the maid answered as she came into the living room.

"I'll be late tonight. Will you leave some lights on?"

"Yes, ma'am."

Carley nodded. She knew Abby would have been thoughtful enough to leave a light or two burning, but Carley had needed to say goodbye to someone before leaving for the evening. Lonely, she thought condemningly. Too lonely. "Good night, Abby."

"Good night, Mrs. McKay."

She went into the vestibule and looked out through the curtains. Arthur and Betsy had offered her a ride to the theater, where the auction was to be held, and as punctual as always, Arthur was just pulling into her drive.

As Carley slid into the backseat, she cheerfully said, "Hello, Arthur. Betsy, I like your dress."

"Thank you," the woman said coolly. "It's not new."

Carley had no answer for that and was instantly reminded of the reason she seldom accepted a ride with them. She had hoped this evening would have been different, but knew she was deceiving herself. As usual Arthur and Betsy would have almost nothing to say to each other, and the silence among them would feel strained. Had she not wanted some company, even this, she would have driven herself. Determined to make the best of things, Carley asked as Arthur pulled out into the street, "Did Eddie win his baseball game?"

"Yes, twelve to two," Betsy said. "And Rosalie has been chosen for cheerleader camp."

"Great," Carley replied with more enthusiasm than she felt. She still wasn't accustomed to having grandchildren old enough to be in middle school.

"Arthur tells me you're doing Chester Goode's latest play."

"That's right. I guess you've heard I have the lead."

"Yes, I heard."

Carley felt chastised and wondered if Betsy had meant to sound so abrupt. "Are you coming to see it?"

"I doubt it. I don't care for musicals, and Eddie has a birthday party to attend that weekend."

"I didn't realize your schedule was so full." Yes, she thought, I should have driven myself.

"The Howard Addamses have asked us to sit with them," Arthur said. "I hope you don't mind." Belatedly he said, "Of course, you're welcome to join us."

"That's quite all right. I've already made plans to sit with Stacy and Bill." Actually she hadn't, but she wasn't going to let Arthur put her in the awkward position of tagalong, and she was certain Stacy and Bill wouldn't mind if she joined them. She hoped Apple Tree's lone taxi would be operating that evening so she wouldn't have to endure a repeat of this at the end of the evening.

When they arrived at the theater building, Betsy looked around and with a frown said, "No one is here yet. Why did you say we should come so early, Carley?"

"I wanted to be sure everything was ready. Arthur said it was all right with him."

"Arthur would. I hate arriving so early everywhere we go. I feel foolish standing around with no one to talk to."

Carley suppressed a sigh and resisted Betsy's subtle invitation to argue. She wasn't going to play Betsy's game. Not again tonight.

Arthur let the ladies out in front of the building, then parked across the street. While they were a few minutes early, they weren't actually the first to arrive. The theater president, Ken Boudreaux, was already there, along with his wife and her mother. They were arranging floral baskets in the lobby. Carley spoke briefly to them and went into the auditorium. Betsy and Arthur greeted the Boudreauxs as if they were the closest of friends—which they were not—and stayed to talk with them.

The padded, removable seats had been stored, and with the exception of an area set aside for dancing, the room was filled with long dining tables, each covered with snowy linens and decorated with an attractive centerpiece. The theme this year was summer rain, in hopes, as Melissa said, of breaking the drought. Colorful umbrellas were arranged along the paneled walls. Fluffy cotton clouds hung suspended from the tall ceiling, and a glimmering rainbow arched across the stage. On the stage were the items to be auctioned.

Carley critically inspected the merchandise, double-checking to be certain each one was tagged with a number and that all were attractively displayed.

As people began arriving, Carley circulated from one group to another, exchanging greetings. Soon the catered food for the buffet dinner arrived, filling the room with delicious aromas.

"We have a good turnout," Stacy said as she and her husband, Bill, joined Carley.

"Now if we can get everyone to bid, we'll do just fine."

Bill grinned at the two women. "I brought my checkbook. That salt block bust of Lincoln would be great for Stacy's next birthday."

"Don't you even think about it," his wife warned.

"She would probably prefer that mount of glass slag," Carley teased. "It's the perfect color to go with her new curtains."

"Is that what that is? Glass slag?" Stacy asked. "Where would someone get a thing like that?"

"See?" Carley said. "I told you she would be interested."

When the line for the buffet began forming, Bill invited Carley to join him and Stacy as she had hoped they would, and she gladly accepted.

As they joined the line, Stacy said to Bill, "I hope Billy doesn't give your sister any trouble tonight. She wasn't too thrilled to baby-sit on a Saturday night."

"Quit worrying," her husband said. "We almost never go out. Enjoy yourself."

Stacy shook her head as she laughed. "I guess it's time we had another baby. Bill says I'm like a hen with one chick."

Carley smiled. The subject of motherhood also made her rather uncomfortable. She wondered if she was becoming peevish and whether that was yet another stage of widowhood.

The food was as good as banquet food could be. The salad was reasonably crisp and the hot foods relatively hot. For the price everyone had paid for their tickets, she had hoped for more flavor, but she heard no one complaining.

The table centerpieces were pots of ivy with long, luxurious runners and were decorated with tiny umbrellas and streamers of colored ribbons. Silver confetti, presumably intended to symbolize raindrops, had been liberally sprinkled over the white cloths.

"Shelley did a great job with the decorations," Bill remarked. "This took a lot of work."

"She's been setting it up for days. You'd think this was a grand ballroom rather than a theater auditorium."

"Removable seats make it so versatile," Carley agreed. Her eyes swept over the crowd. "Have you seen Melissa?"

"She's not coming. I called to see if she wanted to borrow my blue chiffon, but she said she finally got her car out of the shop and she was going to Dallas this weekend to visit her mother."

"I'm sorry she won't be here," Carley said, then felt instantly guilty at the wave of relief that passed over her. She wasn't sorry Melissa wouldn't be coming; she was glad, for that meant Jordan most likely wouldn't come. Carley tried her best to keep her mind on the conversation at the table, but thoughts of Jordan Landry returned with every lull.

Finally the meal was cleared away, and the auctioneer took his place on stage. One by one the items passed across the block and were sold, and the bidding and the auctioneer's antics thankfully kept Carley's full attention.

"What are you going to do with that thing?" Stacy asked as Bill bought the pile of melted glass slag.

"Give it to your mother, of course." He pretended to wince as she elbowed him in the ribs.

Carley bought a set of plastic Kewpie dolls and presented them to Bill. He retaliated by buying her an art deco statue of a nude with a clock in her stomach.

Gradually the stage was emptied of all its treasures and white elephant items save one. The auctioneer brought forward the easel that held a poster for the Bahamian cruise. A hush settled over the crowd as it had for all the nicer items. Several of the active bidders smiled encouragingly at Carley, and she smiled back. Everyone knew the bidding would be brisk, and in the end Carley's premium bid would be the winner.

With a nod to the auctioneer she opened the bid at seven hundred dollars. A satisfied murmur passed through the crowd. Someone in the back raised the bid by fifty dollars, and Carley nodded when the auctioneer asked her to top it.

Again her bid was raised. Carley glanced over her shoulder to see who was bidding, but the crowd blocked her view. When the bidder in the back raised the bid to 950 dollars, several people curiously craned their necks in an effort to see who Carley's competition was. However, she refrained from doing the same because she disliked being so obvious. She motioned to the auctioneer again.

"Eleven hundred," a man's voice said clearly.

"Twelve hundred," she countered. This was almost twice the retail price, but Carley didn't want to lose face. She *always* was the highest bidder.

"Thirteen hundred," the voice said calmly.

"Who *is* that?" Carley demanded to Stacy.

"I can't see him."

His voice was awfully familiar, she thought as she nodded to the auctioneer.

"Fourteen hundred," the man said before the auctioneer could ask. The crowd murmured with interest and speculation.

Carley drew a deep breath. "Fifteen." She had already spent a great deal that evening in order to insure the theater group would have enough money from the proceeds to get the needed lighting equipment.

"Sixteen." With things becoming so spirited with the bidding, the crowd parted so the bidders could face one another. When Carley saw it was Jordan sitting back in a folding chair, looking as relaxed as if he were home on his own front porch, she almost choked. When their eyes met, he smiled lazily.

She didn't want the cruise all that much, and if she had, she could have booked herself on one for half that amount. "Seventeen!" she ground out.

"Eighteen." Jordan's smile told her he wouldn't be outbid.

Carley opened her mouth, then snapped it shut. With a decisive shake of her head she told the auctioneer she was out of the bidding.

"Wow," Stacy marveled. "There must be a better legal business in Apple Tree than I ever guessed. After that, I'm sure we'll have more than enough to pay for the lights and then some."

With an effort Carley made her lips smile. Leave it to Jordan to do this to her.

"I wonder who he plans to take with him," Stacy continued.

"Who cares?" Carley said. "Our theater will have new lights, and that's all I care about." Had he intended to make a public spectacle of her? She wouldn't put anything past him.

"Maybe he plans to take Melissa," Bill suggested.

"I guess I'll be going," Carley said abruptly.

"So soon? It's only ten o'clock." Stacy looked surprised at the idea.

"The dancing is starting, and I'm no good at solos," Carley said in an attempt at lightheartedness.

"May I have this dance?" the familiar voice said from behind her.

She drew a deep breath to steady herself and slowly turned to look up at Jordan. "No."

He grinned as if she had said yes and took her bag from her and laid it on the table. Taking her hand, he drew her to her feet.

"I said no," she objected.

"I heard you."

The band was playing a waltz, and Carley was swept onto the dance floor, her pale green skirt floating gracefully about her slim legs. Jordan was an accomplished dancer, and she found her feet moving in perfect rhythm with his.

"You always used to dance barefoot," he said as he looked down at her.

"The wife of a bank president always dances in heels," she replied in a withering voice.

"Ah, yes. For a minute, I forgot I was dancing with royalty."

"There's no need to be snide."

"No? Then why are you?"

Carley glared up at him. She was all too aware that they were the object of much interest. "Why did you bid so high on that cruise? You must know it's not worth that."

"I know. It will go for a good cause. We can't perform a play in the dark."

"You could have simply donated the money for the lights."

"That wouldn't have been nearly as much fun."

She wanted to say something really nasty, but the words failed her. She had never had to bandy words with Edward, and she was out of practice.

As soon as the music ended, she turned to leave, but Jordan caught her arm and pulled her back into his embrace as a slow song began.

"Turn me loose!" she snapped.

"Smile, everyone is watching."

A glance told her he was right. They were the only couple on the floor. She didn't smile, but she quit struggling and let him lead her into the dance. Other couples joined them. "Do you enjoy embarrassing me?"

"Since when do you get embarrassed by dancing?"

"Since you came back to town. We're the subject of all the gossip."

"There's nothing to talk about," he countered.

"I know that, but nobody will believe me." When she noticed two pairs of accusing eyes staring at them from the edge of the dance floor, she groaned.

"Now what?"

"Arthur and Betsy are over there. Don't look at them!"

"Why? What are they doing?" he asked with interest.

"I guess I can expect another visit from him tomorrow and another lecture on propriety."

"He's your stepson; tell him he'll be grounded if he misbehaves."

Carley glared up at him. "That's not funny."

"No? I think it is."

"Only because you don't have to listen to it. Arthur is still upset that I have the lead role in this play. What will he say about us dancing together?"

"Why do you care what Arthur says?"

"Look, Jordan, it's easy for you. You can just pick up and move away if you decide you don't like it here. I can't."

"Yes, you can."

"I've lived here all my life!"

"And the magic spell of Apple Tree keeps you bound to this enchanted spot? Give me a break, Carley."

She frowned. What he said was true. She really could leave. It wasn't as if she couldn't afford it or she would have to find another job. "People who live in Apple Tree either leave as soon as they are grown or they never leave at all. You know that."

"So start a new trend."

"What are you trying to do? Talk me into moving away?"

"Not at all. As a matter of fact, I wouldn't like that."

His statement startled her. "Why?" she demanded, curious.

"Because you're so much fun to pick on."

Jordan smiled broadly, and for an instant she saw the impish grin of Jordan's youth.

At this, she returned the smile. Jordan had always been a teaser. Even as a small boy, he'd been a downright pest. Memories of their childhood together melted the icy barrier around her heart. "Remember the time you dyed your mother's poodle green?"

He chuckled. "It was just cake coloring, but it took forever to wear off."

"Your mother was really upset."

"I know, but I think the dog enjoyed it."

As she laughed aloud with Jordan, a warm glow spread throughout her, melting her defenses.

"You're beautiful when you laugh."

Suddenly, her smile vanished. "Don't do that." Jordan had touched her heart with those words, and an alarm had gone off.

"Don't do what? Pay you a compliment?"

"I don't believe your compliments," she said in an effort to rebuild the wall he had broken through, the wall that had protected her from pain all these years.

"At one time you did."

Carley stopped dancing and pushed away from his embrace. He had no choice but to follow her off the floor. "That was a low blow, Jordan."

"I didn't mean for it to be."

"No? It seems to me that you've been aiming low blows at me for weeks!" She was regaining her strength to keep him at bay, even though a part of her screamed that it was wrong for her to do so.

"Maybe that's because you've become so thin-skinned since you learned to dance in heels."

"See?" she said as she whirled to face him. "You did it again!" She turned and stalked away.

Right on her heels, Jordan said, "You aren't leaving, are you?"

"I certainly am!" she threw over her shoulder. But then she remembered she had ridden over with Arthur and Betsy, and she stopped abruptly. It was all Jordan could do not to stumble over her. Carley turned to him to speak. Only a breath separated them. "Can I borrow a quarter?"

"What for?" he replied incredulously.

"I need to call the taxi, and our box office is locked. I'll have to use the pay phone in the lobby."

"I didn't think I saw your car outside."

"Will you give me a quarter or not? I'll pay you back at rehearsal next Tuesday."

"I can spare a quarter," he replied dryly.

"I wasn't sure after you bid so much on the cruise."

"Now who's being snide?" He took her arm and said, "I'll drive you home."

"No, thanks. I'd prefer the taxi."

"You know perfectly well he usually takes the weekend off."

"Maybe I'll get lucky."

Jordan walked her to the table where she'd been seated and handed her bag to her. "Good seeing you, Stacy, Bill."

"You're leaving?" Bill asked.

"Together?" Stacy blurted out.

"He won't give me a quarter to call the cab. Do you have any change?"

"I may have." Bill reached in his pocket, but Stacy punched him.

With her most innocent smile, Stacy said, "Sorry. We're all out of quarters."

"Thanks, pal," Carley said with a threatening look at her friend, but Stacy continued to smile.

"What luck," Jordan said as they headed for the door. "Here's Arthur." He went to the man and said, "I'm driving Carley home."

"I don't think—" Arthur began.

"I knew you'd understand," Jordan interrupted blithely. "See you around."

Carley preceded him to the door, her heels making staccato clicks on the floor. "You didn't have to make such a production out of it. It's only a ride home."

"I know. That's all I offered."

He led her to his car and opened the door for her. "I know how to open my own door," she added.

"I assumed as much. Are you going to get in or would you prefer to run alongside the car?"

Carley slid in and watched as he went around to the driver's side. "You can really be a pain. You know that?"

"So I've been told. Primarily by Cindy, though she put it more graphically."

"I'll bet she did," Carley muttered.

"She was very imaginative when it came to language arts."

"I really don't want to talk about your wife."

"Ex-wife," he corrected.

"Whatever." She made the word drip venom.

"I don't want to talk about your ex-husband, either."

"Edward died. That doesn't make him an ex."

"I guess you're right. Your late husband, then. I still don't want to talk about him."

"Good. Then don't bring him up."

"Oh? You don't like to talk about him, either?"

She gave him an exasperated glare. "Turn in the next driveway on the left."

"I know where you live."

"You do?" She waited, but he didn't elaborate.

"Nice house. I've always liked it. Is it really a Frank Lloyd Wright?"

"So I'm told."

"Maybe you could show me the interior sometime."

"Look, Jordan, I—"

"No, not tonight. Thanks, but I'd rather do it another time."

"I wasn't offering you a guided tour."

"Aren't you nervous in there all alone?" he asked as he parked and turned off his headlights.

"Certainly not." She hoped she sounded convincing. Frequently she woke up in the middle of the night and lay in the dark trying to convince herself she was safe and alone.

"I guess you learned that when you learned to dance in heels."

"Thank you for the ride," she said in a cool voice.

"I think we should get together soon."

Carley stared at him through the darkness, unable to read his face. "Whatever for?"

"To go over our lines. In Houston we often met to practice other than at rehearsal."

"This isn't Houston. We do it differently here."

"I still think we should. I mentioned it to Bob, and he said it was a good idea."

"I don't think so."

"You have to admit our duet is still rough in spots and the second act falls apart."

"I don't have to admit any such thing."

"In Houston we never put on a slipshod performance."

"Neither do we, and if you mention Houston again, I'll scream."

"Why would you want to do that?" he asked innocently.

"Again, thanks for the ride." She reached for the door handle.

"Which one is your bedroom?"

"I beg your pardon?" she asked frostily.

"Your bedroom. With most houses I can figure out the floor plan from the outside, but this house goes every which way."

"You have no business knowing where my bedroom is."

"Mine is in the back of the house. It overlooks the lake."

"Jordan, I don't want to discuss bedrooms with you." She could have bitten her tongue. The conversation was far too personal, and she was only making it worse.

"Okay. Do you have a pool?"

"No, I don't."

"That's too bad. If I lived here, I think I'd put one in."

"Build your own pool."

"I have the lake to swim in. It's not as civilized, but there's no upkeep."

"Civilization has never weighed very heavily on you," she retorted.

"We aren't going to talk about Cindy. Remember?"

"I was referring to your personality."

"I seem uncivilized to you? In what way?"

She closed her lips firmly. She could hardly say it was his pagan-god charisma in the moonlight or the way his storm-hued eyes seemed to be daring her to play his word games. "I don't like you."

"That's hardly a news bulletin. You've gone out of your way to make that clear."

"I've done no such thing! My manners are better than yours!"

"Maybe, but if I'm so uncivilized, that's not saying a great deal, now is it?"

"Jordan, what do you want from me?"

He was silent as he studied her. After a long time he said, "I'm not sure."

For some reason this made her feel close to tears. "I've done everything I know. I've avoided you, I've tried to ignore you, I've tried to pretend you're a stranger. What else can I do?"

"You could try being nice to me." This time his voice held no teasing note at all.

"No, I can't. Not with all we meant to each other."

"Carley, I told you I was hoodwinked into marrying Cindy. She even told me later that Kevin wasn't mine. She needed a husband, and I was handy."

"I thought we weren't going to talk about her."

"She keeps stepping between us."

Carley opened her door and drew in a deep breath of the hot night air. "There's nothing between us at all."

"Now you and I know that's not true."

With the interior car light on, she could see him clearly. She was silent for a long moment, then said, "There can never be anything between us."

"Why not? We're both of age and unencumbered. I don't want to get married again, but we could at least be friends."

"No, we can't." Her voice rose. "Don't you see how that's impossible? We've shared too much love for me to just be your friend!" Her eyes widened as she realized she had said too much.

He gazed at her, his eyes soft with remembering. "You're right. There was too much love for us to settle for friendship."

"And I don't want to be anything more. And don't tell me nothing else was offered! I don't live in a cocoon."

He made no reply.

Carley rubbed her forehead. Her jumbled thoughts were giving her a headache. "I don't have affairs, Jordan. I'm not that sort of person."

"What sort has affairs? It's no longer the dregs of society. Nice people have close relationships outside of marriage these days. Especially if they are single and don't want to become...encumbered."

"Marriage doesn't have to be an encumbrance."

"We also weren't going to talk about Edward."

"I wasn't."

She looked across at him and found he was studying her as if he were trying to memorize her features. She didn't need to do the same with him. Every detail of this man was already firmly implanted in her mind. "I have to go in."

Without another word, Jordan got out and came around to her door. Rather than getting out on her own, she had waited for him to help her, hoping the extra few seconds would help her regain her composure.

She took his offered hand and as she slid out and stood next to him, she was uncomfortably aware that because of the heat, her dress was clinging and that Jordan had noticed it. For a moment they stood so close that she could feel the radiant warmth of his body, then she stepped around him and headed for her door. He joined her, matching her step for step. As they went up the porch stairs, her elbow grazed his and she felt the electricity all through her.

In her nervousness, she fumbled with the key getting the door unlocked, but then hesitated before opening it. "I said too much," she murmured. "Forget what I said."

"I don't think I've ever forgotten a single word you said to me."

Her eyes met his, and her heart began to pound even faster. The moonlight limned the strong planes of his face, and in the shadow his hair was an inky thatch. His eyes seemed to be gazing into her soul. Her nerves bristled with his nearness as they thrummed for his touch.

Slowly he bent toward her. A breath away from her lips he stopped, and their eyes asked questions that their lips couldn't voice. Carley closed her eyes and lifted her face, bringing their lips together.

She hadn't intended to do this. She knew she shouldn't kiss him, but she could no more stop herself than she could stop the stars from shining.

His lips were firm and warm, but soft. His breath was sweet in her mouth. Carley's lips parted, and she swayed her body to his as he drew her close. As his tongue tasted her mouth, a thousand feelings burst into life. Feelings she thought were dead or at least buried. And all the feelings were for Jordan and for him alone.

He tasted familiar. He tasted like passionate summer nights and long days in the cooling shade. He tasted so good.

Carley's arms were around him, although she didn't remember putting them there. His body was hard with sinewy muscle. The years hadn't added an ounce of fat to his lean frame.

He knotted his fingers in her hair, and she felt the clips come loose, but she didn't care. All that mattered was the passion he was awakening in her. And the other, more glorious sensations. Sensations she didn't dare acknowledge.

At last he drew back and gazed down at her as he held her face between his hot palms. His eyes, as dark as his hair in the moonlight, burned with a primitive craving. Carley was unafraid. She felt the same craving rushing through her veins.

Jordan reached past her and pushed open the door. The golden light of the hall spread over them. Carley waited, too proud to repudiate the words she had spoken in the car.

With a lazy smile, Jordan stepped back. "Good night, Carley. I'll call you about getting together to go over our lines."

She felt as if he had punched her in the stomach. As he turned and stepped into the darkness, she heard him whistling. Quickly she stepped into the house so he wouldn't see her anger, and only years of practice at controlling her emotions kept her from slamming the door.

Chapter Seven

More iced tea?'' Carley asked Melissa as they sat in Carley's morning room.

"I believe I would like some. My goodness it's hot out there, and it isn't even noon."

"I've never seen such a dry summer," Carley agreed. "I forgot to water my flowers on Wednesday, and by Friday they were wilting. If we're already rationing water in July, what will August be like?"

"I know. My flowers are all dried up. I guess it doesn't matter, though, since I'm moving."

"You are for sure? I was hoping you had changed your mind."

Melissa shook her head. "I can't stay in that house. Even if I don't leave town, I want to move. I put it on the market a couple of weeks ago."

"I haven't seen a sign out front."

"There isn't one. I saw no reason to further antagonize Jack."

"He doesn't know it's for sale?"

"It's in my name. I bought it before we were married, and the payments have been out of my separate checking account."

"I see." Carley poured tea for them both and sipped it as she gazed out over the lawn. Thanks to her sprinkler system, the grass had stayed green, but the trees, which needed a soaking rain, looked tired and listless. "Have you heard from Jack?"

Melissa glanced at her, then quickly looked away. "Not really."

"That's probably for the best. I was worried that he might retaliate when you changed the door locks."

"He might have if I hadn't." Melissa added a spoonful of sugar and stirred her tea as she said, "Jordan has agreed to handle my case on a sliding fee."

"Oh?" Carley tried to sound casual and only mildly interested.

"I think it's very generous of him, since I can't afford to pay his regular fee." She paused for a minute, then said, "Carley, are you still interested in him? Romantically, I mean?"

Carley was silent for a moment. "Of course not. All that was between us ended long ago."

"Stacy said Jordan drove you home from the auction last Saturday."

"I made the mistake of going with Arthur and Betsy, and you know how they are. As soon as we got in the door, they went their way, and I went mine. I was ready to leave before they were. I didn't have a quarter to call the taxi, so Jordan offered me a ride home. He didn't even come in."

Melissa nodded. "Joe Don went fishing last weekend, so the taxi wasn't running anyway."

"It seems to me a town this size ought to have a reliable cab service."

With a shrug Melissa said, "Everybody has a car or can get a ride with friends. Joe Don says it's not worth it."

"Anyway, that's why Jordan drove me home."

"That's a relief. I was worried that I might be stepping into your territory. . . with Jordan, I mean."

"You shouldn't be so nice, Melissa. I'm afraid people will take advantage of you."

"I just didn't want to do anything to mess up your relationship. That's why I asked."

"I had assumed you and Jordan were already dating."

Melissa smiled, and her face lit up. "I'm to meet him for lunch at noon. It's not really a date, but I'm looking forward to it. Besides, until my divorce is final, I would feel odd going on a real date."

"I wouldn't. You can bet Jack isn't sitting home alone."

"He never sat home when we were living together, so I'm sure you're right."

Carley managed to smile. "I hope you have a good time. I really do. Melissa, I don't know how to say this, but don't let him hurt you."

"Hurt me?"

"Emotionally, I mean. You're so trusting. Sometimes I think you're one of the few innocents left in the world."

"I guess that's true. I do always think the best of people."

"There's nothing wrong with that. It's just . . . oh, I don't know how to put it."

"Don't worry about me, Carley. Jordan won't do anything to hurt me."

"No? He hurt me, you know."

"But that was years ago. Everyone changes in time. Haven't you?"

Carley nodded. She had changed a lot from the high school cheerleader who believed in happily ever after.

"Well, so has he, I'll bet." Melissa's lips curved sweetly. "Do you know what he did? He offered to follow me home after rehearsals."

"Why would he do that?"

"Sometimes I'm nervous about going into a dark house."

Carley nodded. "So am I. Abby always leaves a light on when I'm out."

"He's so sexy! If I were playing the part of Alice, I would never be able to remember my lines."

"Yes, you would. Melissa, I'm really going to miss you. Is there any chance you'll stay in town?"

"Not unless something changes." She glanced at the chrome-and-glass wall clock. "I have to run. I'm meeting Jordan in ten minutes."

Carley walked her to the door and said goodbye. She knew what Melissa meant. If things developed between her and Jordan, she would stay. Carley didn't want her friend to move away, but she just couldn't encourage her involvement with Jordan Landry. It wouldn't be in Melissa's best interests. By Melissa's own admission, she hadn't had a real date yet, and how could he be interested in Melissa after the way he and Carley had kissed just the Saturday before? But then, didn't this mean Jordan hadn't changed at all? The pattern seemed too familiar. It was as though this might be a repeat performance.

Jordan looked up with a smile as Melissa joined him at his table.

"Sorry I'm late." She looked around the room in awe. "I had heard how nice Carver House was, but I've never been here before."

Jordan glanced around the room. "They've done a good job in turning the house into a restaurant. The food is good, too." When they gave the waiter their order, Jordan said, "Any more phone calls from Jack?"

"I've been getting a lot of prank calls lately. Heavy breathing and that sort of thing. It's probably Jack or one of his friends." She frowned slightly. "Last night I thought I heard someone outside, but it could have been a dog, I guess. That's what I told myself, at any rate. Whatever it was walked up to my window and just stood there."

"Did you call the police?"

"I was afraid to get up. On these hot nights I sleep with the windows open, and if it had been a person, he could have seen me if I had gotten out of bed. The phone is in the living room," she added.

"If you had a long cord, you could take it into the bedroom with you."

"I don't know how to install one."

"I could do it for you. Do your screens latch securely?"

"Yes. I'm sure of that. Even before Jack left, I was alone a lot at night, so I put screen door latches on all the screens. They can only be opened from the inside."

"That's good. I can put in that phone cord for you this afternoon, if you like."

Melissa cast him an angelic smile. "I'd really appreciate it."

"Your court date is set for July 20, by the way."

"So soon? That's great. What time?"

"The court convenes at nine, but I don't know how many cases are on the docket. We'll just have to go to the courthouse and wait until your case is called. With any luck at all, we'll be finished with everything before noon."

"Then I'll be single again. It seems odd to think that. You know? Like the past five years didn't happen."

"I think everybody goes through a sense of unreality during a divorce. I know I did."

"That's right. I had forgotten. Do you ever regret it?"

"Not for a minute. I should never have married her in the first place." He fell silent as the waiter brought their food to the table. If he hadn't married Cindy, he would certainly have married Carley, and would probably still be married and happy. Unbidden, the memory of her kiss, as sultry as the night, sprang into his mind. He should have asked if he could come in. She might have said yes. On the other hand, she might have been baiting him into exactly that so she could turn him down. Jordan had wondered about that ever since. Cindy would have done such a thing; would Carley?

"This is good. I haven't had smothered steak in ages," Melissa said as she tasted her food. Changing the subject, she said, "It's a shame you didn't have children. At least there would have been something good to come out of your marriage."

Jordan didn't reply.

"That's one of my biggest regrets," she continued. "I let Jack convince me not to have a baby."

"Someday maybe we'll both have children," he said. "It's not too late for either of us."

"You like children?" Melissa leaned forward with interest. "So do I. All my life I've wanted a big family. I was an only child and it was lonely. Seems like I've spent most of my life being lonely. I think that's why I married Jack in the first place—so I'd have someone of my own." She laughed wryly. "What a mistake that was!"

"Loneliness is a bad business," Jordan agreed. "I've had my share of it, too." Especially, he thought, since returning to Apple Tree. In Houston he had stayed so busy that he had overlooked how lonely he was inside. Apple Tree, however, had few diversions. Most of his nights were spent reading or watching TV or simply listening to the house creak. Seeing Carley at rehearsals only served to show him how alone he was the rest of the time.

"I had a couple look at the house yesterday who are very interested. They're newlyweds, and it would be perfect for them if they can get a loan."

"Then you'll definitely be leaving as soon as the play is over?"

Melissa lowered her eyes and gave a delicate shrug. "I guess. I'm not all that anxious to leave town. I just don't want Jack to harass me."

"I can understand that."

"Carley says she wishes I would stay."

"So do I," Jordan said with a smile. "Would you like dessert?"

"Oh, no. I'm full."

He wondered why she appeared to be so shy all at once. Maybe, he decided, it was the meal. Carver House wasn't expensive compared to the restaurants he had frequented in Houston, but she seemed in awe of it. He motioned for the waiter to bring him the bill.

As he put a gold credit card on the waiter's tray, Jordan said, "How are your lines coming along?"

"Just fine. I'm embarrassed to be having so much trouble with such a small part, but some of the lines in act three are so similar to the ones in act one that it confuses me."

"Well, you've had a lot on your mind." He signed the receipt and put the credit card back into his wallet.

"What are you doing this afternoon?" she asked unexpectedly.

"I have to finish my preparation for a case that goes to court tomorrow, then at three a couple of clients are coming by the office. Why do you ask?"

"Nothing. I just wondered."

"I can come by before supper to install that phone cord."

Her eyes lit up. "You'll stay and eat with me, won't you? At least I can do that much to repay you."

"I'd like to, but no thanks. I need to get home."

"Okay." Her voice held a tinge of disappointment, but she smiled. "Maybe next time."

"Sure thing."

As they left the restaurant Jordan glanced at the table by the window where he had sat with Carley. If he asked Carley out, would she accept? Or would she laugh at him and spread it all over town that she had turned him down?

When Jordan realized he must be frowning, he promptly replaced that expression with his attorney's poker-faced facade. He had to stop expecting every woman to be as mean-tempered as Cindy.

He saw Melissa to her car, then drove to the local hardware store and bought a telephone extension cord. Installing it would only take a matter of minutes and would go a long way toward ensuring his client's safety. From what he had heard around town, Jack Thompson was the sort to get revenge. While he was there, he also bought several boxes of nails for a project of his own.

Jordan pulled off his shirt and tossed it over the porch railing, then buckled a leather tool belt around his lean waist. Whistling, he went down the stone path to the lake, where he was building a gazebo. He wasn't sure just where the idea had come from, but one night as he sat on the porch going over his lines, he had looked down at the lake and decided it was a perfect spot for a gazebo.

The building was as Victorian in design as his house, and when it was finished, it would have gingerbread under the overhang, a railing to match the one on the house, and a copper weathervane on top. From it, Jordan would have a spectacular view of the sunset over the water and of the rolling hills beyond.

He put a board in place and began to pound in a nail. The physical activity felt good. Jordan liked to stay fit and missed having an athletic club handy where he could work out on a regular basis. For a minute he considered offering to repair the loose ceiling board on Melissa's porch, but decided against it. She was moving soon, and the porch wasn't unsightly. The new owners could fix it.

His muscles flexed as he lifted another board into place. Melissa had behaved in a peculiar way when he was installing her phone cord—almost as if she expected him to say or do something he hadn't. Poor thing, he thought. She had been so badly victimized by her husband that she was probably leery of having any man in the house. That was a shame, he reflected, because she was such a good person. Maybe in Dallas she would find the kind of life she deserved.

The sun was low, and shadows were gathering under the trees. Crickets sang for rain as if their lives depended on it, but their efforts hadn't been very successful. Overhead the sky was clear, and the few clouds Jordan could see were thinning on the western horizon.

Jordan's father had been a carpenter, and after summers of working on the older man's crews, Jordan was skilled at his work. Maybe, he thought, he could even make his own gingerbread on the lathe in the barn. That would keep him occupied for hours. If he made the design complicated enough, he might be able to banish Carley from his mind most of the time.

There she was again. Carley seemed always to be there at the edge of his thoughts. He had been trying to banish her from his mind when he got the idea to build the gazebo, yet every time he pictured himself enjoying it, his thoughts went to Carley. She had been with him every step of the way.

Jordan paused and gazed out over the water, thinking how wise it had been to put the gazebo on pilings here at the deep end of the lake so it could double as a diving platform. In the shallowed water beneath the walkway that connected the gazebo to the land, he saw a school of minnows gather, then dart away. The setting sun was casting opalescent hues over the wispy clouds. This was a lonely time of day.

In Houston he would have been arriving home. He remembered how Kevin had run to greet him, his thatch of blond hair whipping back from his grinning face. Kevin had been a happy boy. Jordan was positive about that. His life had been short, but he had enjoyed every minute of it. Their love for Kevin had been the only thing he and Cindy had had in common.

Whenever Jordan thought of Kevin, he had the urge to have another child. Not that anyone would ever take Kevin's place, but Jordan had enjoyed every aspect of fatherhood. Even diapers and midnight feedings hadn't daunted him. He enjoyed children, and this house was designed for a family, not a bachelor. Had that been in his subconscious when he decided to move back? he wondered.

Carley had always wanted a large family, too, and she was also childless. She was thirty-three now, just as Jordan was. He didn't think that was too late to start a family, but if she did, kids could be adopted.

He straightened with a frown. What was he thinking of? Carley wouldn't even agree to meet him to go over their lines for the play, much less marry him. Marriage? The furrows in his brow deepened. He didn't want to get married, but this time the idea didn't seem so distasteful as it usually did. Not when he thought of it in relation to Carley.

That was a thought he definitely wanted out of his head. He had been burned by marriage before. If he wanted a family, he could adopt one. Single adoptive parents were still somewhat rare, but not unheard of these days.

But he did want to see Carley. He wanted to see her a great deal. He couldn't get rid of the memory of her kiss. Unless he was mistaken, she had been moved by it, too. Certainly she had responded as if she was. The remembrance of her lips, so soft and sweet beneath his, left him aching inside. With determination he went back to work.

"Carley? This is Jordan." He rubbed the towel over his damp hair, then tossed it into the bathroom as he shifted the receiver to his other ear.

"Yes?"

"We talked about meeting to go over our lines and our songs. Remember?"

"I remember you mentioning it. I don't recall having agreed."

He went to the chair beside the windows and sank into the cushions as he propped his feet on the ottoman. "I thought you had. Anyway, I was wondering about tonight."

"Tonight? You mean now?" She sounded startled.

"Do you have something else planned? I figured Monday night would be pretty slow in Apple Tree."

"It is. It's just that I . . . I mean, I didn't expect you to want to come over tonight."

"Then you have other plans?"

"No, not really. I mean, there's this movie on TV . . ."

"I'll tape it for you. What channel?"

"I can tape it myself."

"Okay. What time should I come over?"

"I . . . well, I suppose now is as good a time as any. It's already eight-thirty, you know."

"Yeah, I know. It got dark outside."

"What does that have to do with it?"

"I was working outside, and it got too dark to see what I was doing, so I came in and called you."

"I see."

"So this is a sudden idea for me, too. It's not like I thought of it earlier and just now got around to calling."

"I guess that's supposed to make a difference?"

"It's not as though I'm calling for a date. I really need to practice my lines." He heard her sigh. It had been a mistake to call so late, but he hadn't been able to get her out of his mind.

"All right. Come on over. I'll put on a pot of coffee."

"Great. I'll be there as soon as I get dressed." He hung up before she could change her mind.

Carley heard the phone go dead. Slowly she hung up the receiver. Get dressed? Did that mean... The thought of his lean, muscular body made her pulse quicken. No, she decided firmly. It was only a figure of speech.

She looked down at her jeans and T-shirt. She looked awful! And her hair!

Carley headed for the stairs at a run. On the nights when she was home alone, she didn't bother with nice clothes or makeup.

By the time she reached her bedroom, she had stripped off the T-shirt and was unzipping her jeans. How long would it take him to drive over here? Five minutes? Fifteen? She dumped her clothes in the laundry hamper and dashed for her closet. Ruffling through her clothes, she discarded one after another. This one was too old; she would look as if she hadn't changed at all. This one was too dressy; she would look as if she cared too much. Time was ticking away.

She pulled out an apricot silk blouse with a lace collar and buttoned it with trembling fingers, then grabbed the matching skirt and wrapped it around her waist. She was in such a rush that her fingers fumbled over the buttons, causing further delay. Why was she so nervous, she demanded of herself. He was only coming over to work on their lines. This was no different from a rehearsal at the theater.

But she knew it was. The rest of the cast wasn't here. She would be alone with him in her home.

Carley shoved her feet into her white sandals and grabbed a gold chain off her rack of necklaces by the closet door. Crossing her bedroom, she fastened the chain around her neck and smoothed her collar back in place.

In the bathroom, she pulled the tieback from her hair and grabbed her brush. As she vigorously brushed, she was thankful to see her hair falling into place in soft waves instead of going every which way. Curly hair wasn't all it was purported to be.

Makeup! She stared at her pale face in the mirror. There wasn't time to put much on, and it was just as well, she thought, because in her nervousness she would probably spill it all over her blouse, anyway. Eye shadow, mascara and lipstick would have to be enough.

Just as she was finishing, she heard the doorbell ring. Carley froze. He was here! She glanced in the full-length mirror as she hurried through the bedroom. At least she had been given enough warning to make herself presentable.

At the bottom of the stairs she paused and forced herself to slow down and draw in a calming breath. She didn't want Jordan to have any idea how flustered she was.

Moving as serenely as possible, Carley went to the door and swung it open. He stood there in the porch light, as handsome as Adonis, wearing a deep green shirt and dark chocolate colored slacks.

"Come in, Jordan," she said in her best society voice.

Chapter Eight

Jordan sauntered into Carley's living room and looked around. "Nice," he said.

"Thank you. I did it myself."

Jordan looked amused, and Carley realized how stilted she must have sounded. It had been a mistake to let him come over. "The piano is in the den. This way."

She felt so awkward. She was sure he realized they were alone. All her nerves were strung to the breaking point, and she was agonizingly aware of his every movement. Jordan seemed to fill the room, to be in command of it. She sat on the piano bench and turned the music score to their duet.

From long practice her fingers played the correct melody, and that was fortunate because her thoughts were scattered. Her concentration was inextricably centered on Jordan. After she played it through once, he said, "Let's try it together."

Jordan's clear voice was startlingly intimate in the den, and Carley missed her cue. On the second try she lost her place in the music.

"Stand up. The piano is distracting you. Do you have a recorder in here?" He fished a cassette tape from his pocket. "Bob recorded the score for me. We'll use it."

Carley dropped the tape into the player on the stereo, and her eyes met Jordan's. As he began to sing the love words, she felt a stirring deep within her. This time her voice entered on the precise note, and her tones blended with his in perfect harmony.

"Why haven't you sung it that way at rehearsal?" he asked when they were finished.

"I find it difficult to sing a love song with everyone watching."

"You'll have a larger audience than the cast on the nights of the performances."

"I know. Besides, we have usually argued at rehearsal, and that makes it even more difficult for me." She wished she hadn't said that. It sounded as if she cared whether they argued.

"I would prefer us not to fight so much," he said. "Maybe we could agree to a truce. At least until after the last performance."

"Maybe."

"If we don't believe in our parts, then no one else will, either. You have to *be* Alice."

"Alice is so naive about some things."

"And Buck can't see the forest for the trees. Just the same, this is their story. In spite of Buck's dogged nature I see a vulnerability in him. He really thinks he can make Alice happy, and he wants that more than anything."

"Alice wants happiness, too, but she sees more to life than being Buck's wife. She knows he won't let her be more than that."

"Chester must live in a vacuum if he thinks women want nothing more than security."

"Security is important, but so is being an independent person."

He leaned toward her. "I wonder what would happen if Buck and Alice met a few years later. Whether the chemistry would still be there, I mean."

Her eyes widened. "Let's go over the duet again."

"It's an interesting question, isn't it?" Jordan said as he rewound the tape. "Alice has gone away and tasted city life. Buck has stayed home. She knows now that the rat race isn't all she expected it to be; he feels as if he's stagnating and is ready for some excitement."

"I'm not stagnating," she retorted.

"I was talking about Buck and Alice. Were you drawing a parallel between them and us?"

"Start the tape." She found it difficult to open her mouth, but once she began to sing, her notes rose and fell in perfect unison with his.

They ended on a note that left Carley's lungs bursting for air. She gulped in a breath, but found herself unable to look away from Jordan's eyes. The silence filled the room.

"Did you hear something?" she asked.

"No." He stepped nearer, and his eyes were smoky, as if he planned to kiss her.

The muted sound rumbled again. "There!" Carley said. "Can that be thunder?" She abruptly headed to the back door and stepped out onto the patio, glad for an excuse to break the spell between them.

Jordan followed her. "Maybe the drought is over at last." As if on cue, a flash of lightning lit the sky. After a moment the thunder followed.

"Maybe it's just heat lightning," she said. "Maybe it doesn't mean anything at all."

"Heat lightning makes no sound. There's a storm brewing."

Carley felt as if she had a storm of her own building inside herself. He was standing so near her that she could feel his breath in her hair. "I guess you should be getting home before it breaks."

"My windows aren't open, and I won't melt if I get wet."

She turned and looked up at him. Lightning flashed again, lighting his face, and she was reminded of some ancient warrior. A warrior who was about to claim his rights. Carley swallowed. "I guess we ought to rehearse some more, then."

"We could do that. Or we could sit and talk."

"What do we have to talk about?" She looked away in confusion. The first of the winds lifted the limp leaves of the pecan trees.

"We have a lot to talk about. I know you feel something when we're together. After all we meant to each other, you have to."

"No, not a thing."

"You never were very good at lying, Carley."

"No?" she challenged as she faced him again. "But you were! You made me believe you loved me, and all the time you were shacking up with Cindy Lou Wallace!"

"That's not the way it was. I was with Cindy once, and only because you said you never wanted to see me again. I was young and stupid for doing what I did, but I did love you! I've never forgotten you."

The thunder growled around them, and more lightning bit at its heels. Carley didn't know what to say.

"I want you, Carley. God knows I've tried not to, but I do. I dream about you every night, and you won't stay out of my mind during the day."

This was the moment she had ached for during all those long years—the moment of her revenge. Yet now that it was here, and he stood vulnerable before her, all she could feel was her pounding heart, and all she could think of was how much she wanted his arms about her. "I want you, too," she heard herself murmur. No, her logical mind shrieked. You're doing it all wrong! But she couldn't help herself. Not when he stood so close and looked at her that way.

"Carley," he whispered, as if her name were an endearment.

Slowly he lowered his head and touched his lips to hers. Carley felt his kiss all the way down to her toes. As he became bolder, a warmth started to build in her middle, then spread throughout her body.

When the first fat drops of rain spattered on their shoulders and the patio, Jordan put a protective arm around her. "Come inside."

They went back into the den, and just then the storm broke in earnest. The drumming of rain coupled with thunder and lightning set Carley's nerves even more on edge. "It's really coming down out there."

"Are you still afraid of storms?" he asked.

"Of course not," she answered a bit too quickly. The thing she feared most at the moment was having to look at him after the kiss they had shared. "Let's go over the duet again."

"Look at me, Carley." He gently lifted her chin and drew her face toward his. When he saw the terror in her eyes, tenderness stole over his face. "You're safe, Carley. I'm here."

"I'm not sure which frightens me more—you or the storm," she said truthfully.

"You aren't afraid of me. You're afraid of yourself."

"Nonsense." She tried to pull away, but he put his arms around her.

"You're afraid that I may make you feel too much. You said you want me, and I want you. There's no one to hurt if we come together. No one is standing in our way."

"We aren't animals, Jordan. There's more to life than just...coupling!"

"Coupling isn't what I had in mind. I was suggesting we make love."

She couldn't breathe, and her mouth was dry as cotton. "I...I can't...."

Suddenly the lights flickered, then went out. Carley instinctively leaned toward Jordan's protective bulk.

"It's just the storm."

"I know. The lights go out in most storms. They'll be back on soon." Her voice was trembling, and she wondered if he noticed.

"Didn't I see some candles on the bookcase?"

She nodded, then realized he couldn't see her. "Yes. The matches are in the container beside them. Like I said, the lights go out fairly often, so I keep them on hand."

In the flashing lightning Jordan made his way to the bookcase, struck a match and lit two of the fat yellow candles. As a mellow glow filled the room, Carley relaxed a bit.

"Better?" Jordan asked.

"Yes. Thank you."

He picked up both candles and moved toward the stairs. "Is this the way to your bedroom?"

Carley clasped her hands nervously. Yes, her mind shouted. "Just because the lights went out is no reason to..."

"I was going to ask that, anyway."

Carley stared at Jordan for what seemed to be a long time, her heart pounding more fiercely with each crash of thunder. Gathering her courage, she said, "Yes. That's the way to my bedroom." She moved toward him, and he stepped aside so she could lead the way. As they mounted the curving stairs, the light from the candles cast leaping and wavering shadows on the wall, while the sporadic lightning brilliantly lit the house one moment, then abandoned it to near darkness the next.

They reached the top of the stairs and Carley pushed open a door. "This is my room."

Jordan stepped in and looked around. Carley's bed dominated the room. It was a modern four-poster with square acrylic posts soaring up from the corners like art deco obelisks. Lace panels were draped over the canopy, softening the cool austerity. The bedspread was of white lace, and mounds of lace pillows were piled against the headboard. The windows lent an unobstructed view of the backyard and the storm.

Jordan put the candles on the dresser and went to the windows. That end of the bedroom was cantilevered away from the house, and he felt an uncanny sensation of floating above the ground. With the storm raging outside, it was exhilarating. "Come over here, Carley. This is great!"

"I'd rather not."

He turned to find her standing near the door, her face drawn and frightened. Jordan went to her and put his arms around her. "If you're so frightened, why do you live here alone?"

"It's just the storm. Normally it doesn't bother me at all to be here. This is my home."

He held her quietly. He knew Carley, and he didn't believe her. She wasn't a loner.

"Besides," she continued, "I like my privacy. With parking in the rear of the house, no one knows if I'm alone or even if I'm here."

"I know. That's where I parked."

She looked up at him in surprise. "You did? Why?"

"Folks in Apple Tree love to gossip. Your neighbors might not know I came here to rehearse our lines and songs. It's nobody's business if I'm here or not." He paused, then said, "Is there someone else who usually parks in the back?"

Slowly she shook her head. "No."

Jordan smiled and ran his fingers through her thick hair. It felt so soft and silky. Just the way he had remembered it. And fragrant. Her hair always smelled faintly sweet as if it were freshly shampooed. At one time he had teased her about it. Now he only wanted to luxuriate in its scent and texture. "You know," he said, "you've always had the prettiest hair I've ever seen."

"Jordan, what about you? Is there an extra car parked behind your house some nights?"

He shook his head. "Only my own."

He saw her relax a bit, so he drew her to the window. "Look at it, Carley. It's fantastic! All that raw power unleashed for us to enjoy. It's like a magnificent fire-works display.''

''I never thought of it like that. Tornados are more what I connect with storms.''

''Let yourself enjoy it. This is nature's passion.'' He always felt such exhilaration in storms that he wanted to impart some of it to her. ''This is a great room to see it from.''

''Is that why...''

''Look at that strike! I haven't seen lightning like this in years!'' He glanced down at her. ''I sure can't im-agine Edward McKay in a lacy bedroom like this. Look! Twin flashes!''

For a minute Carley wasn't sure she had heard him correctly.

Jordan's eyes met hers. ''Was he the sort to go in for lace and frills?''

''I redecorated,'' she said testily.

Jordan looked back at the storm. She was surprised to see what could only be jealousy on his face. ''This was my room. Edward's was down the hall.'' She saw a faint smile touch his lips. ''This is a big house. He said there was no reason for us to crowd each other.''

''I don't think I would feel crowded if I were sharing your bedroom.'' The lightning flashes cast stark shad-ows and lights on his strong features. ''I don't think you would find it crowded, either.''

Carley didn't know how to answer that because she knew he was right. ''Edward had his interests, and I had mine. We had a good marriage, but we were never close friends in the sense you mean.''

''I didn't think so. That's necessary, you know—to be friends.''

"Not always. It depends on what sort of marriage you're interested in. Sometimes respect is enough."

"Not for me. Oh, sure, respect is part of it, but I want friendship, as well."

"Were you and Cindy Lou friends?" For some reason the storm had given them an amnesty, a common ground where they could speak their minds freely.

"No. No, we were never friends. We were never anything but married."

Carley put her arm around him. "That's sad. In a way I wish you had been happy."

"Oh?"

"And in another way I'm glad you weren't."

He smiled and pulled her close. "At last I see my Carley. Honest to a fault."

"I've tried hard to get rid of that Carley."

"I can see how she wouldn't fit into the bank president scene. Personally, I find her adorable. I always have."

Carley gazed into Jordan's eyes, and her pulse tripped faster, this time not because of the storm. "Did you want to come up here just to have a better view of the storm?"

"No." His voice was deep and caressing, touching chords within her that responded eagerly.

"Kiss me," she whispered. In the roar of such a tempest there was only room for truth, and the truth was that she not only wanted him, she needed him.

When his lips met hers, she put her arms about his shoulders and let her fingers run through his hair. He tasted so good! Desire poured through her, leaving her weak, yet exhilarated. "Make love with me, Jordan," she whispered.

He bent and lifted her in his arms, and in that moment she felt safer than she ever had in her life. Cradled against his hard chest she could feel the thud of his heartbeat. She felt secure, and she felt desired. Carley hadn't experienced much of either in a long time.

Jordan carried her to the bed and let her body slide down his until her feet touched the carpet. His arms held her against him so that their bodies were melded together. Once more he bent and kissed her as if he were determined to enjoy every second of their loving.

Carley knew this was a truce and not an end to their war. She knew nothing had changed between them and that he had not said a word about love. Tonight, though, that didn't matter. She had loved him long ago and had never really stopped. Her love for him was her secret as it had been for so many years, but tonight, in the oasis of truth provided by the storm, she could have him. She didn't allow herself to think further than that.

He caressed her neck, then gently felt for and found the swell of her breasts. He fingered the first button on her blouse. Carley felt his touch in every atom of her being. The first button gave way, then the second. She saw a muscle ridge in his jaw and realized he was exhibiting great restraint.

When he reached the waistband of her skirt, his fingers released the buttons as if he had already memorized the way to do so. "I've wanted to do this all night," he said softly. "To see you standing like this with your eyes so soft and gentle."

"I don't feel gentle," she replied. "I feel like the storm out there."

"So do I."

He let the skirt swirl down to the floor as he brushed her blouse down to join it. His eyes grew darker as he unfastened her bra and pulled it away. "God, you're beautiful. You're like a goddess."

Carley, who had never heard words being spoken during lovemaking, felt the love blossom within her. "When I saw you in the storm, I was reminded of some sort of ancient warrior. A Saracen maybe. One that was barely civilized and very sexy."

He smiled, and his face became more tender, though the desire for her never left his eyes. "I feel barely civilized right now. It's all I can do not to throw you down and ravish you." His fingers trailed over her soft flesh until he reached her breasts. Cupping one in each palm, he said, "You feel so good!"

Carley unbuttoned his shirt and pushed it over his shoulders. He was more powerfully built than she remembered. Sinewy muscles ridged his stomach and fanned across his chest. Dark hair curled beneath her hands as she caressed him. His skin was fevered with wanting her, and she felt his barely leashed passion in the tautness of his muscles.

He waited while she fumbled with the unfamiliar intricacies of his belt buckle. She raised her eyes as it came free in her hands. "Jordan? Are you sure we're doing the right thing?" She found it difficult to talk when his hands were setting her on fire.

"If you have any doubts, tell me now." His voice was husky with desire. "Do you want me?"

"Yes," she whispered. "Oh, yes!"

Jordan removed the rest of his clothes as she turned down the covers on the bed. When she knelt on the cool sheets, he lowered himself beside her. His body told her that he did indeed want to make love with her.

Carley laid her head on his shoulder, and her body molded naturally against his. "We fit as if we were made for each other," she said.

"Perhaps we were. Maybe I was born for you and you for me." He held her close and caressed her back from her shoulders to her buttocks. He slipped his thumb under the elastic of her panties and eased them down and off her legs.

"Carley, you don't know how often I've dreamed of this." His words were almost drowned out by the thrumming of her heart and the raging of the storm.

"I've dreamed of it, too," she confessed. "Especially since you returned to Apple Tree."

"Then you thought of me before, as well? You fantasized about having me here in your bed? Of my touching you like this? And this?"

She closed her eyes as he gave her pleasure, and she nodded because she was unable to speak. She had fantasized that he would be doing exactly these things, but in real life it was far more exciting than she had imagined.

He nudged her legs apart and found the bud of her sensuality. Carley drew in her breath sharply as pure ecstasy flooded through her. "Jordan," she murmured. "That feels so good."

"I love to touch you. To feel your body respond to me."

It was true. Her body sang to his touch and her senses were tuned to every nuance. The sound of his voice thrilled her in symphony with his caresses. She wondered if she would ever get enough of him.

Jordan continued to strum her with his fingers as he lowered his lips to her breast. She felt the warmth of his breath, then the tingling sensation of his tongue on her nipple. A soft sigh escaped her parted lips, and she arched her back to offer herself more fully to him.

"You like that?" he asked, his voice as smooth as velvet. "How about this?" He closed his lips over her nipple and sucked gently as his fingers continued to stroke and tantalize.

No man had touched her in such a long time. In the last years before Edward's death, sex had been only an occasional occurrence. Carley felt her body responding with an urgency that was almost frightening. She'd never made love with a man so young, so strong and so virile. He was a consummate lover. He knew instinctively where and how to touch her and what would give her the most pleasure.

All at once Carley felt her desire racing, then she clung tightly to him as shattering waves of ecstasy swept through her. She knew it felt especially good because it had been so long, but then it was so much more. She'd never felt such a release as this. When she opened her eyes, her chest still rising and falling with her rapid breathing, Jordan was smiling down at her. "That's just the first one," he said.

His knowing fingers began to stroke her again, and Carley's eyes widened. She had not expected more, had never had more and started to tell him so, but already her body was quickening and she couldn't talk.

This time when she reached her peak, he slid inside her, filling her, and the sensation of becoming one with him was so overwhelming that she cried out. She held to him as her body arched against him in pure pleasure.

Jordan held her closely as if he were fighting hard to control himself. "You feel so damned good," he murmured as he began to move within her.

Carley couldn't speak. Not when her body was already calling out for him again. She wanted to tell him she had never felt this way before, to tell him no one had ever awakened her like this, but words were inadequate to describe the wonders of his lovemaking.

She matched her rhythm to his as naturally as if they had always been lovers. Jordan lifted his head and gazed deep into her soul, his eyes as dark as a storm-filled sky. Carley raised her head and claimed his lips in a kiss that was as wildly passionate as the sensations he had awakened. Again, with an intensity that touched the core of her being, she reached her fulfillment. The rhythmatic waves triggered his own, and she felt him thrust deep inside her as he joined her in the culmination of their loving.

For a long time she stayed in the cradle of his arms, afraid to speak or move for fear she would shatter the spell. She loved him. It was as simple as that and as complicated. Of all the people in the world she could have chosen to love, he was the worst possible candidate, but there it was. She loved him.

Carley opened her eyes and found him watching her. "You're beautiful," he said.

"I never felt anything like . . ."

He put his fingers to her lips to silence her. "There's no one in the world but you and me. There never has been."

She smiled the gentle, sensuous smile of a woman who has been well loved. The storm had passed, leaving a steady rain that encased the house like a silver cocoon. "No one," she whispered. "No one at all."

She wondered what he would do now. Never having made love with a man who wasn't her husband, she wasn't sure what might follow. Would he get up and go home? Go downstairs for a beer and TV?

Jordan cradled her head on his shoulder and stroked her hair as he put loving kisses on her forehead. Carley drew her leg up between his thighs and curved her arm over his side. As contented as lovers could be, they slept.

The sound of the doorbell dragged Carley from her sleep. She moved slightly, and her muscles twinged. Her bare leg touched warm flesh, and her eyes flew open.

Sunshine poured into the room, gilding Jordan's tanned skin. His dark hair was tousled, and his cheeks were stubbled with an overnight growth of beard. As she stared at him, he opened his eyes and smiled.

"You're still here!" she said.

"Good morning."

The doorbell sounded again, and Carley clutched the sheet to her breasts as her eyes widened. "Who could that be?"

"How should I know?" he said with a laugh as he stretched. "I don't live here."

Carley grabbed her bedside clock and exclaimed, "Nine o'clock!"

"You had a busy night. No wonder we overslept."

When the doorbell persistently rang again, Carley swung her legs over the side of the bed.

"Maybe if we ignore it, they'll go away," Jordan suggested.

"Who could be coming over here now?" she worried as she tried to pull the sheet free. It stayed firmly anchored. "I can't just ignore it. Everybody knows I'm always home this early in the morning." She gave up on the sheet and crossed the room to the closet.

"You go see who it is. I'll just lie here and enjoy the view."

Carley looked back to see Jordan watching her, and she blushed. She had never slept naked before in her life. Even though they had spent most of the night making love, she was embarrassed for him to see her in the daylight. She grabbed a caftan and jerked it over her head. "You stay here. Don't make a sound. Okay? I don't dare let anyone know you're here. I'd be embarrassed to death."

Jordan's smile quickly faded. "Whatever you say."

As she ran barefoot downstairs, Carley combed her fingers through her hair, wishing she'd had time to smooth things with Jordan. She hadn't meant to be so abrupt. She was just shaken at having an unexpected visitor. Did she look as sexually satisfied as she felt? Surely the long hours she had spent in Jordan's arms must have marked her in some way. She didn't feel like the same person.

She yanked open the door and felt as if ice water had been poured over her. "Arthur!"

"Hello, Carley. Sorry to wake you up, but I thought you were an early riser."

"I am. I mean, I usually am. Arthur, what are you doing here?" She was all too aware of her nakedness beneath the caftan and of Jordan upstairs in her bed. Arthur had never looked more like his father than he did to her now.

"I was on my way to the bank and thought I would drop off these papers for you to sign. Just business as usual." He brushed past her and into the living room.

Carley's thoughts were in a turmoil. Would Jordan be quiet and stay out of sight? Was this Abby's day off, or was she about to come in the back door? Carley felt disoriented and bewildered. She couldn't possibly let anyone know Jordan had spent the night. In minutes it would be all over town!

"Where do I sign?" she said hurriedly. She had to get rid of Arthur and fast. She didn't trust Jordan to do as she'd told him. Maybe he had had something like this in mind all the time! "Give me your pen."

Arthur produced his pen, and Carley all but snatched it from him. Her fingers were shaking so much she could hardly produce a passable signature.

"Is something wrong?" Arthur asked. "You seem so nervous."

"You woke me out of a sound sleep," she said. "I'm not fully awake yet."

"I wanted to talk to you about your rental property," Arthur said as if he had all day to discuss it. "Now, the commercial buildings are holding their own, but some of the houses are starting to show their age. I suggest you sell the older ones before they need repair and invest in some newer ones. That's what Betsy and I are doing, and I think—"

"You're absolutely right, Arthur. I was just thinking that the other day." She edged him toward the door as she said, "Why don't you take care of that for me?"

Arthur looked pleased. "I'm glad to see you're taking my advice for once, but we have to discuss each property. I can't—"

"You're right again." She took his arm to propel him faster. "I'll come down to the bank this afternoon, and we'll go over each one. Say at two o'clock?"

"That'll be fine." He gave her a perplexed look. "I'll see you then."

"Bye now." She shut the door behind him and leaned against it to catch her breath. After a moment she recalled what day it was. Luck was with her; it was Abby's day off.

She lifted her eyes to the ceiling. Now what was she going to do with Jordan? All her senses urged her to go back to bed with him; all her logic told her she had made a big mistake. He had never once said he loved her or anything of the sort. He hadn't even suggested that last night was anything other than a one-night stand. She felt sick at having wanted him so much as to lose all her objectivity. With his inflated ego, he must think she would be his for the asking.

She ran up the stairs and found him finishing dressing. His face was dark, and the shine had left his eyes. "I'd better go," he said in a strained voice. "I wouldn't want to damage your sterling reputation." His eyes fell on the photo of Edward on her dresser, and his frown deepened.

It was just as she'd thought it would be—character assassination, as usual. "Well, it *is* sterling," she snapped. "This isn't a city where people can come and go in bedrooms with nobody caring one way or another!"

"An interesting turn of phrase, considering how we spent the night."

Carley blushed scarlet. "I didn't intend that as a double entendre."

He gave her a typically maddening smile.

"I have a good name in this town, and I don't want it damaged!"

Jordan crossed the room so fiercely that Carley backed into the wall. He planted his hands to either side of her head and glared at her as he said. "There aren't many women who would consider it demeaning to have spent a night with me. If I recall correctly, you didn't object at the time. You needn't worry about your precious reputation, because as far as I'm concerned last night never happened!''

He jerked away and strode down the stairs before Carley could gather her wits enough to speak. ''Jordan! I didn't mean—''

''Goodbye, Mrs. McKay! Thanks for an interesting evening!'' He stormed out the front door and slammed it so hard that the windows rattled.

''Damn!'' Carley exclaimed. ''Well, damn!'' It wasn't having spent the night with him that embarrassed her, but rather in having been caught by Arthur with a man in her bed. ''You're a pigheaded fool, Jordan Landry, and you always have been,'' she shouted at the closed door.

That made her feel a little better, so she said it again. ''Just a pigheaded fool.'' And a damned good lover, she added silently.

Then she went back to her room to look for solace, but found only emptiness. When she noticed Edward's picture on the dresser, she put it away in a drawer. He no longer figured largely in her life. Pushing back the tears that were welling in her eyes, she decided to soak in a hot bath and try to pull herself together.

Chapter Nine

Jordan drove home, his thoughts on Carley. Now that he was away from her and was able to think more clearly, he knew he had overreacted to her concern over embarrassment. Carley did that to him. She made him feel protective and irritable all at once. She seemed to magnify all his emotions. When he was around Carley, he was on a mental roller coaster.

Logic told him that Arthur had no right to know he had spent the night with her. Jordan didn't want anyone to know because of the aspersions it would cast on Carley's character. But in some primitive, territorial, uncivilized corner of his mind, he wanted every man to know—to know she was his woman so they would stay away from her.

"That's crazy," he muttered aloud as he turned in his drive. He didn't own her. He didn't even *want* to own her. Independence in a woman was attractive to him.

He parked and gazed for a minute at the nearly finished gazebo as a half memory tugged at him, then vanished. The gazebo was attractive, but why had he ever wanted to build it? Carpentry wasn't one of his primary interests.

With a shake of his head, Jordan went inside. He had an appointment at ten-thirty, and he would have to hurry to keep from being late.

As he showered, he thought of Carley and how they had made love throughout the night. She had been so responsive, so giving. Jealousy blazed unreasonably in him to think another man had taught her the secrets of love. Or had he? Even as a teenager Carley had been able to rock him to the soul with her kisses. Maybe her lovemaking skills were natural to her. That made Jordan feel better. He knew his jealousy was unreasonable in view of everything, but he couldn't help it. Carley had that effect on him.

He shampooed his hair and rinsed it under the shower. The water striking the tile wall reminded him of the rain that had accompanied their lovemaking. He could almost hear Carley's soft murmuring and the stifled cries she'd made when she reached her peaks. And she had reached them so easily. He had never seen such a responsive woman. Just thinking about her made his body grow hard and his senses intensify. They had made love in the true sense of the word, and Jordan already wanted her again.

He turned off the shower and stood there dripping while he considered what to do. He couldn't want her. Carley wasn't the type to be satisfied with a love affair. She would want a commitment. That meant marriage. Jordan frowned. In his experience marriage meant a wife who spent more money than was earned, who

nagged incessantly, who was the opposite of a lover.
"Wife" meant Cindy Lou Wallace.

Jordan stepped out onto the shaggy bath mat and
toweled himself dry. He had managed to survive one
marriage, but it hadn't been easy. He wasn't about to do
such a thing again. Most of the marriages he had observed at close hand—his with Cindy, his parents', his
Uncle Ned's—all had been no more than battlefields.
Surely it would be no better with Carley. Cindy had
been sweet and feminine until after the wedding ceremony. His Uncle Ned had said the same thing about
Aunt Grace. His father had once said all woman were
like that—his theory had been that a wedding band
somehow acted as poison on a feminine nervous system. Jordan wasn't prepared to go that far, but he had
come from an unhappy home and been in an unhappy
marriage. He wasn't at all optimistic about the wedded
state.

Despite his intentions to concentrate on business and
not Carley, she kept popping into his mind. His three-
thirty client's perfume, the color of a stranger's hair, a
turn of phrase common to all long-term inhabitants of
Apple Tree, and there she was. Her smile beckoned him,
and he could almost hear the silver music of her laughter everywhere he turned.

By the time he was dressed for rehearsal that evening, his nerves were abraded, and he was terribly irritable. Not enough sleep, he told his body. Not enough
loving, his brain corrected.

He saw her car parked opposite the theater door, and
his breathing quickened. He was as eager to see her as
if he were a boy again who was in the throes of first
love. How would she react when she saw him? Would
she use the subtle signals and intimate tone of voice that

women used to show other women that a man was taken? Did he want that? He wasn't sure.

There was no one else he was the least bit interested in, but Jordan wanted to be the aggressor. At least until he had had time to decide if he wanted a permanent commitment. It could embarrass them both if Carley staked out her claim on him and they'd never made that commitment. Jordan wasn't at all sure he could ever bring himself to that point again, and Carley could lose face with all her friends. Better to play it cool, he counseled himself. To take it slowly and see how the relationship developed. He thought he loved her, but couldn't it just be hormones and a remembrance of their love in the past? A wise man wouldn't rush into anything.

Carley looked up as Jordan entered the theater. Her nerves had been jangled all day. Even the simplest of decisions had been too complicated. Her mind had wandered so that Arthur had actually been angry with her and had insisted that they do their business another day.

Jordan was so handsome, she thought as he came down the aisle. Any woman would be excited over that face and that body. And he made love as if he had invented the activity. A warm blush crept into her cheeks. She had never known it could be like that. Making love with Jordan had been more exciting and satisfying than her favorite fantasies.

Then she remembered how angry he had been when he'd left, and she frowned. A man in love wouldn't leave angry, would he? At the time she had been convinced Jordan had actually wanted Arthur to know he was there in her bedroom. If he cared about her, wouldn't he be eager to protect her reputation? She had heard how men enjoyed passing along stories of their conquests. Had Jordan spent the day doing that? Again the blush returned, but this time it was painful.

She saw Jordan pause to talk to Bob, who looked in her direction. They exchanged a laugh, and Bob gave Jordan's shoulder a comradely whack.

Carley whirled and pretended to be busy arranging the props on the side table. Logically she knew Jordan had not just told Bob how he had spent the night, but the exchange had appeared pretty peculiar. Maybe Jordan had given Bob the details earlier and was just reminding him. Would he do that?

"Carley?" Bob called out.

She reluctantly stepped toward the director as Jordan went around to the stage steps. "Yes?"

"Jordan tells me you practiced your duet last night."

A cold fist seemed to grip Carley's stomach. She nodded.

"I can't tell you how glad I am. Sounds like everything went great. I'm glad you two are working out your problems. It's important for you to make Buck and Alice believable for the audience."

Carley's mouth dropped open. Jordan had told! Worse than that, he evidently had made love to her in order for their characters to work better on the stage! Rage built within her to the point she heard a dull roaring in her ears. He had used her! And he had told Bob! Who else had he told? The fury snowballed until she had to clench her teeth to keep from screaming.

"Act three," Bob said. "Let's take it from the top."

If Jordan wanted realism, she would give it to him, Carley thought as she took her place.

Jordan glanced at his script to get his lead-in line, then stuffed it in the back pocket of his jeans. He went to the screen door to make his entrance and gave her a sexy smile. Carley tossed her head and turned her face away.

Jordan rapped on the door, and Carley crossed the stage to open it. "'So it's you,'" she snapped.

"'Look, Alice, I can explain everything,'" he said with Buck's arrogant swagger.

"'Oh? You think so?'" She let her real anger give emphasis to the words she usually said with cool disdain. "I think you're despicable!" Her eyes flashed, and her skin was chalky as she glared up at him. "'I think anyone who would do what you've done is disgusting!'"

"'Well, what about you, Alice? Don't you think I have any feelings?'" Jordan's voice was as angry as her own, and his eyes were as cold as slivers of steel.

"'I don't care about your feelings, Buck! Not about this!'" Carley used the lines to pour out all the venom she wished she were expressing to Jordan. "'All our lives you've been the boss, but not about this!'" She thrust her face toward his and stepped menacingly closer. "'When it comes to my future, I have to think of myself first.'"

"'You usually do,'" he retorted. "'Don't give me that bull about always putting me first! You're the most egotistical woman I've ever met!'"

"'And you're the most selfish man! I wish I could go away and never see you again!'" Carley's nose was a bare inch from his, and her fury trembled throughout her body.

"'That would suit me just fine,'" Jordan ground out through clenched teeth. "'You just go to that city and pour your heart out trying to get it to notice you, and when you're beaten and broken, you come crawling back to me!'"

"'You selfish pig!'" Carley's voice broke in her anger, and her eyes sparkled with unshed tears. "'I wouldn't come crawling back to you if you were the last man on earth!'"

"'No?'" he asked with stinging sarcasm. "'Let's see you prove it, if you dare. Go on! Leave me! Go to the city!'" His voice dropped to a gravelly threat. "'You don't have the nerve to leave me. Not ever!'"

Carley swung at him in the manner they had carefully choreographed, and Jordan caught her wrist. For a long moment they exchanged a glare that went far beyond the look called for in the script. Then Carley jerked free and ran off the set.

For a minute there was a stunned silence, then the entire cast applauded wildly. Jordan only half heard them. Carley had *meant* those words! What in the hell was going on here?

Bob was grinning like a Cheshire cat. Chester Goode was pacing so fast that his wiry body bounced from foot to foot, and he was wringing his bony fingers as he chuckled and nodded.

"That was great!" Bob shouted. "Carley, come back on stage. You two were great! I never thought of doing that scene in a serious vein. I always saw it as an aloof word play. But said with anger, it really *means* something. Dad-gum, but you two are good!" He nodded his head vigorously. "Let's keep it like that. I know it will be stressful, but I like the emotion you put into it. Good!"

"It won't be hard at all," Carley said with a frigid look at Jordan. "I'm not sure I could play it any other way."

The furrow on Jordan's brow deepened. He had expected her to fawn over him. Instead she acted as if he had insulted her. Jordan had always thought he had insight into human psychology, but Carley didn't fit any of the molds. What kind of woman would make love to a man all night, then act as if she hated him!

A coldness settled around his heart. Maybe he had simply been available when she had needed a man. She had not once mentioned love. She had only said she wanted him. Perhaps any man would have been as desirable at the time. People could change a lot in fifteen years. He no longer really knew her.

The actors went back to their places, and Jordan said his lines to Melissa, who was portraying Alice's mother. Jordan felt every bit as angry and frustrated as Buck should. "'I'll never understand Alice,'" he said in exasperation to Melissa. "'Never as long as I live!'"

Melissa made the correct responses, her normally soft voice cast into the range and cadence of a much older woman.

After rehearsal Jordan felt drained. He couldn't have been more emotionally exhausted if he really were Buck, and if Alice had actually left him in favor of her career. Carley evidently felt the same, he noticed, because she was making a big production out of ignoring him. Jordan knew some actors had trouble putting the characters aside once they were deeply immersed, and he wondered if Carley might be that way. She had certainly been immersed in something! She acted more like his enemy than his lover.

"Jordan, could I talk to you?" a whispery voice said.

He turned and nodded. "What's up, Melissa?"

"I got another phone call just before I left the house. Jack knows when I come to rehearsal and when I get home."

"Did he threaten you?"

She nodded, her eyes wide with fear. "He says such terrible things! It turns my stomach!"

"Why not just hang up on him?" He glanced over to where Carley was talking in an undertone to Stacy. What was Carley saying? Undoubtedly it was something about him. Stacy looked at him, then averted her eyes. Jordan scowled.

"If I ever hung up on Jack, I think he'd kill me," Melissa protested in a frightened voice. "You don't know what's he's like! He can't stand for me to talk back or judge him in any way."

"I'll follow you home."

"Would you? I hate to ask you to do this, but would you come in and check out the house? He threatened to hide inside until you leave. See, he even knows you follow me home. Jordan, I'm so scared!"

"Don't let him get to you. That's what he's trying to do. Of course I'll come in with you. Are you ready to go now, or would you rather go across for coffee with the others?"

"Now, if you don't mind. I'm afraid I wouldn't be good company tonight. I'm so afraid somebody will guess what I'm going through and either feel sorry for me or think I'm weak. I'd hate that."

He walked with her up the shadowy aisle. "You only have two weeks to go and the divorce will be final. Do you want to stay at my house until then?"

Melissa glanced quickly at him, her lips slightly parted.

"It's no trouble," he assured her. "I have several extra rooms. That house was built when large families were common."

"No, thanks," she said after a pause. "I'd better stay at my place. Folks in Apple Tree are so... conservative...that it wouldn't look right if I stayed with you." She smiled shyly. "But I'd like nothing better."

Jordan grinned down at her. Melissa was so sweet. He was as fond of her as if she were his sister. "I know, let's stop off at the grocery store and buy lemons. You can make some of your famous lemonade while I search the house."

"Okay." She looked up at him as if he were the center of the universe, and Jordan felt some of his deflated self-confidence return.

They went to the large new store that had recently been built. Like the others in the chain, it featured twenty-four-hour service. Jordan and Melissa were the only customers. They bought a big bag of lemons, some sugar and a package of popcorn. Jordan kept her laughing and her mind off her troubles. He even drew a smile from the bored and sleepy check-out clerk.

He followed Melissa through Apple Tree's nearly deserted streets and parked behind her in the drive. Melissa made him feel almost macho in her wistful helplessness, and he considered shouting a challenge to Jack in case he was hiding nearby. Good sense prevailed, however, and he followed her into the house.

The small rooms no longer held any secrets from Jordan, and he quickly checked every corner and closet. When he was done, he reported back to Melissa with a snappy salute. "Landry reporting, ma'am. Your house is Jack-free."

Melissa giggled and swept her wispy blond hair over her shoulder as she put ice cubes in two glasses. "Thank you, Jordan. I'd be so scared without you."

"Glad to oblige, ma'am," he said, attempting a John Wayne accent. "I ain't had a shoot-out in weeks. My trigger finger's itchy."

Melissa laughed as she poured oil and popcorn into a skillet. Soon the sound of popping kernels punctuated the air. Jordan went to the refrigerator and got out the butter. He felt at home here. Melissa was easy to be around. For a minute he considered confiding in her about Carley. Not about them making love, of course, but about the mixed signals Carley was always sending him. Jordan had never had a confidante, however, and he wasn't sure how to open up to one.

"Umm," Melissa said as she tasted a buttered kernel. "This is so good! I love junk food."

"So do I. After my divorce I lived on popcorn and candy bars for weeks."

"Then you learned to cook?"

"I already knew how. I had cooked most of the meals the last couple of years of my marriage. Cindy was always too 'tired.' No, I ate junk food because there was nobody there to argue with me, and I could do as I pleased. It was great."

"I hope my divorce goes as smoothly as that."

"Don't get me wrong. No divorce is easy, even when you want one as much as Cindy and I did. We had spent years as a family, and the severing of that bond was really unpleasant. I had to face up to the fact that I couldn't make the marriage work and that our mutual friends were going to be uncomfortable and ultimately would chose sides—they always do eventually, you know. It wasn't pleasant, but it had freedom written all over it.''

"Sometimes freedom can be pretty scary."

"You're telling me. I didn't know how to go about dating or even where to go to meet single women. At least not the kind I wanted to date."

"I've had the same sort of worries," she confessed.

"Don't be too concerned. You'll soon figure out how to get your needs met."

Melissa looked up at him as if she were giving serious consideration to his words. "I almost wish I wasn't moving to Dallas."

"Oh?" He picked up a handful of popcorn.

"Not that I would stay in this house. The young couple I told you about is going to buy it. They'll move in the week after the play. I told them I couldn't possibly move out before then."

"Good idea."

She ate another kernel before she said a bit too casually, "I could get another house here in town, though."

"With Jack around? He won't leave you alone there any more than he would here."

"He might if I had a steady boyfriend."

Jordan smiled. "Isn't it funny how nobody has come up with a good name for grown people who date? 'Friend' has too platonic a meaning and 'lover' has too much. 'Man friend' sounds ridiculous."

Melissa smiled, but her eyes were serious. "You know what I mean."

"Do you have anyone in mind?"

"Actually I do, but I don't think he knows yet. Or maybe he does. I can't tell for certain."

"Whoever he is, he will be damned lucky to have you." He washed the popcorn down with lemonade and reached for more.

Melissa lowered her eyes and began to trace a wet design on the side of her frosty glass. "If you want to spend the night, it would be okay." Her finger paused as she waited for his answer.

Jordan stopped chewing and put his head to one side. "Pardon?" He had heard her clearly, but he couldn't believe his ears.

With a nervous laugh Melissa traced the pattern faster. "Nothing. I was just talking."

Alarms went off inside his head, and apprehension swept through him. He had never considered that she thought of him in a romantic way. He swallowed hastily. "Melissa—"

"No, no," she said with another strained laugh. "I hope you didn't take me seriously."

The alarms clanged louder. She had been quite serious and had obviously expected him to agree to stay. Jordan went to her as she stood and crossed to the sink. Gently he turned her to face him. "Melissa, you're my friend."

She blinked rapidly, and her smile wavered. "Well, I know that," she said in a shaky voice. "Of course we're friends."

He had to handle this carefully or she would be hurt. "Melissa, I find you very attractive. You're pretty and smart and sweet. One of the nicest things about you is that you make other people feel special. When I'm with you, I'm ten feet tall."

"Is there something wrong with that?"

"I'm not ten feet tall. I'm not the one you're looking for. I can't be your knight in shining armor. I have trouble fighting my own battles at times. You need someone who wants to settle down and get married."

"And you don't?"

"And I don't. I'm not sure I'm a good candidate for marriage. I sure as hell botched my first one."

"It would have worked if you had been in love. I don't think any person can *make* another person be happy."

"See?" he said gently. "You're wise and you deserve someone other than me. Someone who loves you the way you deserve to be loved. Not as a friend."

Melissa drew in a deep breath and smiled, but tears glazed her eyes. Silently she nodded.

"I think I'd better go," Jordan said. "Are you okay?"

Again she nodded. "I think I would like to be alone right now."

Jordan went to the door and paused. "I meant what I said about us being friends. If you need my help, you promise to call me. I can be here in five minutes from anywhere in town."

"Thank you, Jordan. I promise. And, Jordan, if you ever change your mind about us being just friends, I'll be here for the next two weeks."

Jordan grinned and winked at her, then left.

All the way home he grilled himself over whether he had given her reason to believe he had ever wanted more than a friendship. He had never meant to lead her on, and he was always careful not to run up false flags. At least he thought he had been. Even if he wasn't falling in love with Carley, he wouldn't be romantically inclined toward Melissa. She was too dependent and emotionally fragile. She was like the spun-glass figures on his grandmother's mantel—pretty to look at but too frail to touch.

By the time Jordan arrived at his house, the phone was ringing. His first thought was that it might be Melissa. He shoved open the door and grabbed the receiver. "Hello?"

"Jordan? This is Bob."

He relaxed against the doorframe. "Hi, Bob."

"I just got home and I couldn't go to bed until I told you again how much I liked act three tonight. I mean when you and Carley went at each other, I thought you meant every word!"

"I'm glad you liked it."

"Liked it? Hell, I loved it! Now if you two can just get that kissing scene down."

"I've been thinking about that. What if we just do a stage kiss? You know, a near miss."

"With all that chemistry between the two of you? No way. Everybody in the audience would know you were kissing the air. I guess this is pretty personal, but, well, do you think you could practice it? I mean, you're both single and all."

"You're right, Bob. That is pretty personal."

"Yeah, guess I shouldn't mention it to you."

"I gather you haven't suggested it to Carley."

"No, I thought I'd sound you out on it first. You know, man to man."

"We aren't going to practice it. I'm sure Carley would never agree to it, either."

"Yeah, probably not." Bob sighed. "Well, there's only one thing to do. We'll go over it in rehearsal until you get it right. That peck you're giving each other will never do. Hell, I kiss my grandmother with more feeling than that!"

Jordan laughed despite himself. "You must have a weird grandmother."

"You know what I mean."

"Yeah, I know. Okay, Bob. You want a kiss, so I'll give you one. Just don't expect it until opening night. Okay?"

"I've got to have it by Grand Dress. I have to see how it looks before you're in the middle of a live performance."

Jordan drew in a steadying breath and said, "I know. Hey, I'm sorry to be this difficult. It's just that Carley isn't the easiest person in the world to kiss in front of the entire cast."

"Humor me. You'll be doing it in front of the whole town in two weeks."

"You've got a good point there. Okay, but if she bites my lip off, see if she's had her rabies shot."

Bob laughed. "Come on, now. Every man in town wishes he could be in your place. Give them something to eat their hearts out over."

"Okay. I will."

"Well, it's late. I've got to get to bed if I'm going to make a living tomorrow. See you at the next rehearsal."

"Bye, Bob." Jordan slowly hung up the receiver. He wanted very much to kiss Carley again, but not necessarily on stage. There was no telling what her reaction might be.

Chapter Ten

You're making a mistake, you know," Stacy said as she sipped her coffee in Carley's breakfast nook.

"About what?" Carley said as she poured herself another cup. This was already proving to be another hot day, and thus she had chosen to wear a mint-green sundress that made her look and feel as if she had her own special breeze.

"About Jordan, of course. You know you want him, so why don't you go after him?"

"I don't want him. Why would you think such a thing?"

"Come on, Carley. I've seen how you look at him when you think no one is watching. He looks at you the same way."

"I don't know what you're talking about." Carley's eyes met Stacy's. "He does?"

"Everyone has noticed it. At least nearly everyone. Melissa hasn't mentioned it."

"That's good. Melissa wants him for herself."

"I don't know about that. Maybe she's just preoccupied over her divorce. It's next week, you know. Besides, he's the attorney who's helping her get out of all this, and she probably feels he's saving her. After Jack, any man who was halfway decent to her would look good." Stacy took another cup of tea. "I saw Jack the other day. He looked awful. Sort of rumpled and dirty like he was on a drinking binge."

"Poor Melissa. I hope he continues to leave her alone. To tell you the truth, I never thought he would. That man is just plain mean. Why do you suppose she ever decided to marry him?"

"I guess he looked better then. Maybe she was lonely or thought she could reform him. Who knows?"

Carley nodded. "I like Melissa. That's part of the problem. If it were Shelley who was interested in Jordan, I might give her a run for her money. But Melissa? She needs all the happiness she can get." The words cost her a great deal, so Carley added, "Even if it's with somebody like Jordan Landry."

"Now there you go again. What makes you say things like that about him?"

Carley sighed and looked out over her expansive green lawn. "I don't know what I feel about him. I really don't."

"And you never will if you don't give him the time of day. It wouldn't hurt you to *talk* to him."

Carley's lips lifted in a wry smile. Stacy didn't know she had done far more than talk to him. Since the night they'd made love, he had scarcely been more than socially polite to her.

"And then there's that kiss scene," Stacy continued. "I know it's none of my business since I'm not the director, but if Alice and Buck are in love, I think they should kiss more passionately than that."

"Sure you do," Carley retorted. "You don't have to do it. A peck on the cheek would be fine with me."

Stacy looked unconvinced. "I think I'd grab him and kiss him until his teeth rattled. At least it would be a good ice breaker."

"I don't doubt that. He would probably chew me out right there in front of everyone." She curled her legs under her and ran her finger along the rim of her cup. "I don't want to 'break the ice' as you put it. I'm perfectly happy with my life just as it is."

"I don't believe you. Carley, you're burying yourself."

"I'm doing no such thing. I have a lot of interests," she protested. "The theater alone takes up hours and hours."

"But that's not a romantic interest."

"The world doesn't revolve around romance, you know."

"Maybe not, but it sure makes it more interesting."

"Stacy, I loved Edward. I don't want another man in my life."

Stacy leaned forward and put her hand on Carley's arm. "Edward was a good man, but he's gone. You're too young to draw back and let life pass you by. Why, I don't think anyone is ever old enough to do that."

"You just don't understand. Jordan is too... complicated. He's not a person I can simply date."

"Oh?" Stacy asked with interest. "Why not?"

"We meant too much to each other at one time. We even planned to get married!" Carley laughed shortly at the bittersweet memories. "We were going to have a houseful of children, a dog, a cat, hamsters. Our house would have a shady yard for the kids, a gazebo for me. We would sit in the gazebo at the end of each day and have time to ourselves to recount the day's trials and triumphs. He was going to be an attorney; I was going to be an interior decorator. We had a full-blown castle built entirely of clouds."

"I think you ought to call him."

"What? Didn't you hear what I just said?"

"Yes, I did, and I think you ought to see if he still feels as strongly about you as you do about him."

Carley put her cup down and wrapped her arms about herself as if she felt a chill. "All right. I *do* care about him. But he obviously doesn't feel the same for me. He barely speaks to me."

"Well, when he does speak, you give him the cold shoulder."

"And then there's Melissa."

"I'm not going to say that all's fair in love and war because she's our friend, but what if he would have preferred you if you only gave him some encouragement? Melissa still plans to move to Dallas as soon as the play is over. All you're taking from her is a week and a half of rebound affection, and you could be gaining something really worthwhile. Melissa is my friend, too, but I can't see her as the wife of a successful attorney."

"I have no more formal education than she does."

"It's not a matter of education. It's a matter of... I don't know, of polish. Melissa would be out of her element. I know that sounds harsh and judgmental, and I don't mean it against her, but I'm your friend, too. Of the two of you, I think you're more suited to Jordan."

Carley was thoughtful for a minute. "Melissa really is leaving town?"

"Her house is already sold."

"I guess I could call him. All he can say is no."

"I'll bet he won't."

Carley reached for the white phone and balanced it on her lap. "I'm scared. Can you believe it? I'm as nervous as if this were my first time to ask a man out."

"Dial his number before you back out. Should I look it up for you?"

"No. I know it." She saw Stacy's smug smile and added defensively, "I happen to have a good memory for numbers."

"Dial it!"

Her fingers felt icy as she punched in his number. On the second ring she heard his voice. "Hello, Jordan? This is Carley."

There was a pause, then he said, "How are you?"

"Fine. I was wondering..." She quickly swallowed the lump in her throat and said, "Would you like to have dinner with me tonight? Say at Rainbow's End on Lake Cherokee?"

Again there was a pause. "Why? Did you lose a bet?"

"There's no need for sarcasm. Forget I asked."

"I'd like to."

"You would?"

"What time should I pick you up? Say, seven?"

"Seven would be fine." Her heart was racing, and her palms were damp. "I'll see you then." She started to hang up.

"Carley? Thanks for calling."

She smiled. "Sure. I'll see you tonight." She met Stacy's triumphant eyes and said, "Thank you...I think."

Rainbow's End was the finest restaurant in the area. Located several miles northeast of Apple Tree near the town of Longview, the restaurant was built over the edge of the lake and had a pier that stretched out over the water. When they pulled up in front, the doorman opened Carley's door as a uniformed parking attendant came around to take the keys from Jordan.

"Nice," he said. "I haven't been here since it was redecorated."

The art deco interior was flamboyant with sleek ebony glass statuettes amid banks of dumb cane greenery. Along one wall, flanked by large, decorative mirrors, was a marble waterfall, and the gurgling water helped mask the sounds of the dining crowd. Everything in the dining room had been coordinated in colors ranging from flamingo pink to soft apricot with glossy black-and-white accents. A stage band was playing in the area with the best view of the water, and in keeping with the decor, the music was mellow and sentimental.

"I love it here," Carley told him. "I wish it were closer to Apple Tree so I could come here more often."

"It's not that long a drive."

"It is if you're traveling alone." Then she added hastily, "Of course I usually come with Stacy and Bill or some other friends."

"Or Edward?"

"Edward never liked it here."

"Maybe it reminded him of his youth during prohibition."

"He wasn't that old, and if you're going to be nasty you can take me back home."

"Sorry. I won't mention him again."

She wasn't so sure she believed him but chose to overlook the barb in hopes the evening would be pleasant. She let the maître d' pull out a chair and seat her.

"Did you order that moon? I'm impressed," Jordan said as he sat opposite her.

Carley followed his gaze to the fat yellow moon that was reflected in the glassy lake waters. "It was included in the reservations."

"I like it."

As Jordan read his menu, Carley pretended to be doing the same, but she was too edgy to pay attention to it. Since Jordan had picked her up, it had been this way—sporadic small talk, long silences, and anytime anything bordering on intimacy was said, one or the other of them cut it short with a rankling comment. She hadn't intended it to be this way. She had hoped for... what? She wasn't sure.

After their orders were taken, another nerve-racking silence ensued.

When Jordan finally spoke, it startled her. "You're really doing a good job on Alice's character."

"So are you, with Buck I mean. I never knew you had a talent for acting."

"I guess there's a lot we don't know about each other. Like why you asked me out, for instance."

Carley returned her gaze to the moon and lake. "I'm not sure, either. After thinking about it, I almost called you back and canceled."

"I'm glad you didn't."

"Why?" she asked bluntly.

He considered for a minute before he answered. "Because we're so good together."

She frowned. "I don't want or need an affair to muddy up my life. I'm not looking for a sex partner."

"Neither am I."

"And I don't want to get married, either."

"Neither do I. So what do you want? A buddy? I don't think we can settle for that. Especially not after the night we spent together."

"I don't know what I want," she admitted with a sigh. "I'm so confused!"

"There is another possibility. We could become lovers."

"I said I'm not looking for sex."

"Lovers are a lot more than sex partners, as you so succinctly put it. They are also friends and companions."

"That sounds like a commitment to me."

Jordan's eyebrows knitted in puzzlement. "Does it?"

"All friendships are commitments. I don't know that I want a lover. It sounds so. . . I don't know. Wrong."

"Only in Apple Tree."

"Well, I'm *in* Apple Tree. Or at least I usually am."

"I wasn't trying to make you angry."

After studying his face, Carley decided he was telling the truth. "Whenever I'm with you, I feel like a firecracker that's ready to explode."

"That's not necessarily so bad. Why not let nature take its course?"

"Because I can't do that. I can't go with my emotions and not give a thought about tomorrow. I can't live for the moment."

"Carley, you have to understand that I have no plans at all to remarry," he said gently but firmly.

"Neither do I. I'm not asking anything like that of you."

"Then why are we here? We both want more than a platonic friendship, but you say you won't be my lover, and neither of us wants a commitment. If you ask me, that only leaves estrangement."

"You're confusing me more than ever."

Jordan leaned forward and took her hands between his. "Haven't you learned by now that there are no guarantees? What you have at any given moment may be all you get."

"That's pure pessimism."

"I didn't mean it that way. I meant that if two people feel the way we do about each other, they would be foolish to throw it away just because they don't like the name for it or because it may not last."

"But what exactly do we have between us?"

Jordan leaned back and released her hands. "You ask hard questions, lady."

"Is it just lust? Don't you feel more for me than that? Don't you think—" Carley abruptly stopped as their waiter approached with their food.

As the waiter served them, Jordan took the time to think. What did he feel for her? It felt like love, but if he said as much, then she would certainly take that as a commitment to marriage. Most women believed you couldn't have one without the other. And if she were one of them, he certainly couldn't tell her he loved her.

"To answer your question," he said when the waiter left them, "I'm not sure. You aren't the only one who's confused."

Carley didn't respond, and as she cut into her steak, he studied her face in the candlelight. Carley had always been the embodiment of all he'd wanted in a woman. He was afraid to do anything to upset the delicate relationship they had. On the other hand, he had quickly tired of cold showers and of working until he dropped in order to sleep. The obvious conclusion seemed to be to make Carley his lover.

"The way I see it," he said carefully, "is that we should go with what we're feeling. You live at your house and I live at mine. We can be circumspect and no one else will know."

"In Apple Tree?" she asked in disbelief.

"It might take some planning, but we could do it. It happens all the time."

"Oh?" Her eyes lit with interest. "Who do you know about that I don't?"

"That's not the point."

"I know it's not. I was trying to change the subject."

"Why can't we discuss this rationally and come to some solution?"

"Because it's too emotional a subject to be discussed as if we were planning a project."

When he realized that he really had been, he felt a twinge of conscience. "I wasn't doing that."

"Jordan, I don't know what I feel, much less what I want to come of it. Of the two men I've ever loved, one left me for another woman, and the other died. I'm not at all sure I want or even *can* trust myself to love again. And that's what it would have to be—love."

After a long moment he nodded. "I know. And I feel the same way. So what do you suggest we do?"

She suddenly realized she had gone too far and was feeling much too vulnerable. In her defense, she said, "I think you should date Melissa and leave me alone."

"Melissa?" he asked in confusion. "How did she come into this?"

"She cares for you. You must know that."

"I also know that she's my client. I don't mix my business and my personal life. Besides, that has nothing to do with you and me."

"I think it does. She's my friend. I see how often you two talk together, and you almost always leave the theater at the same time."

Jordan started to explain, but bit back his words with a frown. He had promised Melissa that he wouldn't tell anyone about Jack's threats. "Melissa and I are just friends."

Carley looked at him as if she were examining his eyes for some hint that he was lying. "Is that really all there is?"

"She's my friend and my client." He felt he could say no more and still maintain Melissa's confidentiality. "You have to trust me on this, Carley."

Slowly she nodded. They ate their meal in polite, but strained, conversation. Carley had hoped Jordan would have a better solution to the problems of the emotions they couldn't seem to suppress. She wondered if he was right that it would be foolish to waste their love on the chance that it might not last. But surely, she thought, something that blazed so brightly as this couldn't possibly continue indefinitely. Surely so much passion would burn itself out and leave her with a guilty conscience. And beautiful memories, her traitorous thoughts insisted.

Carley argued with Jordan over who should pick up the tab since she had initiated the date, and finally they agreed to split the check.

"There's an extra penny left over," he grumbled. "Okay if I pay it?"

"I guess," she replied with a smile. "I'm not unreasonable."

Jordan gave the penny to the waiter and stood to hold Carley's chair. "Would you like to walk on the pier? It's a beautiful night."

She nodded, feeling more confident that she was in control of her feelings. She was sure the night air would help keep her thoughts clear. The combination of wine at dinner and Jordan's presence made her feel more sensuous than logical. That was a dangerous way to feel around him.

They went out onto the pier and strolled down to the far end, their shoes making hollow sounds on the boards. Carley put her hands on the rail and leaned toward the black water as she inhaled the cool air. "I love East Texas," she said with a sigh. "I can't imagine wanting to leave it for a city. Alice is crazy."

"I wanted to leave at one time," he said. "I thought Apple Tree was too small and much too slow paced."

"But you came back."

"I found out a faster life-style and crowds of people don't make that much difference as to how a person feels inside. If you aren't happy one place, you aren't likely to be much happier somewhere else."

"A philosophical lawyer. What will they think of next?"

"So I came back to Apple Tree. I never really left it in my heart. My roots are here. I like the stability of not having a town change its skyline overnight the way Houston does. I enjoy the fresh air and having everyone know my name and for me to know theirs."

Carley looked across the water to the far shore, which was delineated only by a dark smudge of trees. "At times I wonder if I ought to leave, though. To see more of the world than Apple Tree. I've taken vacations, and I've visited some great places, but sometimes I wonder what it would be like to live somewhere else."

"Houston, like every city that I know of, is really a huge cluster of small towns. Each neighborhood has its own shopping area and schools and neighborhood. You have more choice in whether you get to know your neighbors, but it's remarkably the same as a small town in that the boundaries are there."

She turned to face him and leaned back against the rail. "I can't picture you living in your aunt's house. A Victorian house reminds me of lavender and old lace."

"I've made a few changes, but then Aunt Estelle wasn't the lace and doily type. Would you like to see it?"

She hesitated. Was he offering her more than his words implied? After a while she nodded. "Yes, I would." Whatever she felt for him and wherever their relationship was going, she wanted to know.

"You're sure? I don't show my house to everyone, you know."

"Don't you?"

"You're the first person in Apple Tree to have the Landry house tour." He paused and added, "And probably the only one."

Carley felt her pulse quicken. "Then I'm honored that the tour was offered."

His eyes smiled. "Aren't you going to ask what the tour costs?"

She shook her head. "I'm willing to pay the price."

"Let's go."

Her thoughts were racing as they went back to his car. As he tipped the parking attendant, she stared at him. He was so tall and broad-shouldered and handsome. Was it his incredible physical attractiveness that made her feel this way? His charisma? A combination of both? There was an electricity between them that she couldn't deny, whatever its source.

Ever since the night they had made love, she had worked to convince herself that her memory had exaggerated how marvelous it had been. By making love with him again, she could prove that it had been nice, but not as earth shattering as she had remembered. It couldn't be.

As they drove back to Apple Tree, Jordan held her hand and they discussed the play. When she would let herself, Carley enjoyed the intimacy of friendship that was growing between them. Edward had never been interested in the theater, and she loved being able to discuss it with a man and have him understand.

The ride home seemed very short. Soon Apple Tree's familiar scenery surrounded them. As usual at night, the tree-lined streets were deserted.

Jordan's house wasn't very far from Carley's, but in the few blocks between them, the spacing of houses had become farther apart and the lawns increasingly bigger. The streets lights here, casting their golden pools of light, were designed to reflect the style of the Victorian houses they guarded.

As he parked the car, Carley felt a wave of nervousness. She had had no experience in this sort of thing. Was she supposed to stay all night as he had? That would necessitate her wearing her silk after-five dress home in the light of morning, and Abby would be there early. She wished frantically that she had some guideline to follow in matters like this. Why were there no books on how to conduct a successful love affair? she wondered giddily.

Jordan opened her car door, and Carley got out. From that angle, she couldn't see his private lake, though she could feel a cool, damp breeze. The huge oak trees that almost surrounded the yard cast deep shadows. In the golden porch light, she saw a wide veranda, which curved around three sides of the house.

Jordan unlocked the front door, flipped on a light switch, and stepped aside for her to enter. Carley looked about in surprise. "I love this!"

Graceful curves and swirls of gingerbread decorated the high doorways, and the honey-colored oak floors gleamed. Brass pots of luxuriant plants lent a coziness to the entrance and living room. The deep blue walls against the white woodwork and overstuffed chintz furniture were a far cry from the fussy interior she had expected. On the other side of the entry was a curving staircase with a handsomely carved oak rail and massive newel.

"I told you not to expect doilies," Jordan said as he closed the door on the night.

Carley turned to him. "You're a man of many surprises. Until now, I pictured you surrounded by chrome and glass."

"I used to be. This is much more comfortable, I think. I see this old house as a friend instead of just a roof to keep out the rain. It's seen a lot of living."

"I love old houses," Carley agreed.

"Then why don't you live in one?"

She shrugged. "It was too much trouble to move, I guess."

He watched her as she went about the living room, discovering the reading nooks and his crystal collection. She looked at home here, he thought. She fitted in this house far more naturally than she did in her own.

He bit his lip as he considered the track his thoughts were taking. If he was perfectly honest, he would have to admit to himself that he wasn't all that convinced that he wouldn't welcome a commitment with Carley.

After they had explored all the rooms downstairs, Jordan held out his hand to her. Carley's hand was cool in his, and he wondered if she was nervous. He knew he was.

Together they walked up the wide stairs side by side. Would she spend the night? he wondered. He wanted her to. He wanted to wake up and find her beside him in his bed. To make love with her again in the pale dawn light.

His bedroom was painted a deep green that looked even richer against the white woodwork and curtains. His bed was large, and its carved walnut headboard and footboard would have dwarfed a smaller room. For a bedspread he was using a colorful quilt made years before by his aunt. He looked at the room critically, trying to gauge how Carley would see it.

She touched the cushioned arm chair and smiled. "It's beautiful. I feel so... warm here."

"You feel that, too? This house has always been like that to me. I never lived here as a boy, but I visited often, and it always felt like home."

When she came to him, she seemed to be suddenly shy, mildly apprehensive. "Do you want to see the other bedrooms?" he asked.

She shook her head. "Not now."

He gazed down into her dark eyes, and knew her timidity was due to the intensity of her emotions and not because she was regretting having come here. This new depth of feelings made him a bit shy, as well. Whatever his lips might have said, this was no mere love affair.

Without speaking, he drew her into his arms and kissed her. Her body felt so incredibly good next to his. She was exactly the right height and shape, and when he kissed her, he wanted to merge his body into hers until they were one heart and one soul.

As her lips parted beneath his, Jordan ran his tongue over the silkiness of her mouth. At the feel of her tongue, his body responded with desire. Carley's kisses had always sent his senses reeling.

She held him close, and as she pressed her body against his, Jordan cupped his hands on the rounded swell of her buttocks and pulled her even tighter against his hips.

After relishing the warmth of her luscious body next to his for a long moment, he released her and gazed into her eyes as he undressed her. Deep within the shadows of her soul, he saw the love she felt for him and hoped his own eyes mirrored his love for her—a love he was still afraid to acknowledge, but which existed nonetheless.

When their clothes were about their feet, he drew back the bed covers and watched as Carley lay down on his pale blue sheets. For a moment he stood there savoring the sight of her in his bed, with her auburn hair spread like a crown about her face. He had pictured her there so often.

He eased himself onto the bed and gathered her into his arms. Her skin was warm and soft, and her beaded nipples traced fire across his chest before her breast mounded lusciously against him. She kissed him again, this time exploring his mouth with her tongue as he had done to hers. Her fingers laced in his hair, and her body writhed seductively against his.

Jordan shifted, and when he cupped her full breast, his heartbeat quickened. The flesh was firm, yet pliant, and her nipple was hard against his palm as if in supplication to his lips. He lowered his head and closed his mouth over the treasure. Carley sighed with pleasure and edged closer to him. As he bathed the warm bud with his tongue, he fought to restrain the ardor it aroused in him. He already wanted her so badly that he ached deep within his loins, but he would not be rushed. He wanted this precious time they shared to last forever.

For what seemed hours, but could have been only minutes, they mutually explored each other's body, exchanging increasingly passionate kisses and tender caresses. Then, when Carley's hands came to rest on the erect center of his maleness, Jordan felt as if he would explode. Her touch was gentle and hesitant, so he put his hand over hers to let her know he enjoyed what she was doing.

She slipped her leg between his and opened herself to his touch. She was warm and moist with desire. When Jordan felt her responding to his stroking fingers, he pulled his hips forward and they became as one.

Jordan struggled to control himself as her incredibly supple hotness snugly enveloped him, and her hips began to undulate seductively. Somehow he held back as he gave her first one climax, then two more. He wanted to do this all night, to give her pleasure and to hear her soft murmurs and gasps of excitement and to know he had given this to her. At some point, he became aware that his restraint was possible because Carley's gratification was more important to him than his own.

When he knew she was satisfied beyond any shadow of a doubt, Jordan increased the thrust of his hips. As she cried out in pleasure, he let himself enjoy the feel and sound and smell of her, then his own culmination roared through him. As he hugged her tightly, he felt what could be nothing but overwhelming love. She was his woman; he was her man. And he loved her.

Carley had slept in Jordan's arms for hours and wasn't sure what had awakened her. Maybe it had been the warmth of his body beside hers or the unaccustomed feel of his bed, but her eyes were open on the moonlit room, and she was wide awake. She moved slightly, and he rolled from his side to his back.

Slowly she sat up and looked down at him. She had made a big mistake in coming to his house. Maybe Jordan wasn't sure how he felt about her, but she no longer had any doubts about her feelings for him. She loved him. And he had still not said a single word about loving her.

As frustrated tears stung Carley's eyes, she slipped out of bed. She had to get out of there and try to put her emotions in order.

She gathered up her clothes and crept out into the hall, where she hastily dressed in the darkness. Carrying her shoes, she tiptoed down the stairs. He had left a light on in the entry hall, and in its brilliance, she felt exposed, so she hurried out the front door.

As she balanced on one foot, then the other, getting her shoes on, she peered into the darkness. Although nighttime in Apple Tree held no terrors for her, she envisioned everyone she knew driving by and seeing her putting on her shoes under Jordan's porch light.

Fortunately her shoes had reasonably low heels, and she was able to move quickly across his dark lawn. Carley avoided the streets where she might be seen, and instead cut across vacant lots and backyards she had known since childhood. By the time she reached the security of her house, her cheeks were wet with tears, and she was convinced that Jordan didn't love her and never would.

Chapter Eleven

Jordan awoke slowly. At first he couldn't figure out what had roused him because everything seemed perfectly normal. Moonlight glowed beyond the window, and the rest of the bedroom was bathed in velvety darkness. The house was silent, and far away he heard a dog bark. Jordan rolled to his back and felt cool sheets. He reached out and found only a pillow.

He opened his eyes and raised up on one elbow and looked at the indentation in the pillow where Carley had been. A glance told him she wasn't in the bathroom, because the door was open and the room was dark.

He sat up and ran his fingers through his hair. "Carley?" he called out. There was no answer.

With a frown Jordan swung his legs over the edge of the bed. He had driven her here in his car. She had to be here somewhere. He pulled on a pair of jeans and padded barefoot to the hallway. "Carley? Are you down there?" Silence followed in the wake of his words.

Worried now, Jordan hurried downstairs. He had not bothered to turn off the lamp in the living room, and he could tell at a glance that Carley wasn't there. He went through the dining room to the kitchen, but it was dark and empty. So was the den.

He went back to the stairs and looked up at the shadowy hall. "Carley? Are you here?" A glance at the front door told him the dead bolt was unlocked. She must have gone.

Now he was really worried. What could make her leave his bed in the middle of the night? Especially since she had no car to drive home in?

Jordan took the stairs two at a time and crammed his feet into his tennis shoes as he yanked a T-shirt over his head. Carley must have had some real problem for her to leave like that. Had he said something to make her mad? Or not said something that he should have? Maybe she had gotten sick in the night, or frightened. Maybe she had heard a noise, gone down to investigate and had been murdered or abducted!

Jordan's heart was racing as he tore back down the stairs. He ran out the door and onto the brightly lit porch. "Carley, are you out here?" he shouted. The neighbor's dog yapped in reply, but Carley didn't answer.

He jumped off the porch and jogged around the house, even peering down at the lake on the off chance she might have gone for a solitary swim as he sometimes did.

When he came back around the front, he was more concerned than logical. It seemed unlikely that a woman would choose to walk home in the middle of the night when all she had to do was to wake him up so he could drive her. He couldn't imagine any woman doing such a thing in Houston. But this was Carley and Apple Tree. It was possible.

Jordan didn't bother taking his car because he knew the direction she would have taken. He might be able to overtake her if he hurried. He set out in a jog across the dark lawns.

After showering and putting on a nightgown, Carley absentmindedly brushed her hair while studying her reflection in the mirror. In retrospect, she supposed she should have told Jordan she was leaving or at least have left him a note, but at the time she had been too eager to get away so she could think things through. She considered calling him to explain why she had left, but she wasn't really sure herself and she hated to wake him. She certainly couldn't say she had run away because she loved him, especially not when he so obviously didn't feel the same way about her. No, he was just out for a good time, and she had been foolish to read any more into it than that. He had never led her to believe anything else.

Carley put down her brush and turned out the lights as she went to her bed. She had been so foolish to get mixed up with Jordan again. A prudent person would have learned her lesson the first time, she chastised herself severely, but not Carley McKay. No, she had to plunge in like a fool and fall in love with him all over again. The more she thought about it, the more disgusted with herself she became. Jordan was apparently accustomed to sophisticated city women who tumbled into and out of affairs without a second thought. It probably had never even occurred to him that she lacked whatever it was that would allow a woman to do that.

She pulled back the covers and slipped between the sheets. Through the eerie distortion of the lace netting that surrounded her bed, she could see the pale blue of her walls—nearly silver in the moonlight—and the shape of her two overstuffed chairs. When she was decorating this pastel confection of a room, she had been intent only on making a feminine nest for herself. Now it seemed so frilly as to be unwelcoming to a man. Had she subconsciously had this in mind?

She threw her arm above her head and closed her eyes, but as sleep seemed out of the question, she tried to force herself to relax.

Seconds ticked by. Her eyes opened. What was that sound? She listened intently, but heard nothing out of the ordinary, so she closed her eyes again.

Suddenly she heard the muffled splintering of glass, and her eyes flew open as she sat bolt upright in bed. Someone had broken a window!

Carley grabbed the flowing robe that matched her gown and thrust her arms in the sleeves as she stepped into her slippers. Was someone breaking in or was this an act of vandalism? She pulled open the top drawer of her dresser and dug through the piles of scarves and slips looking for Edward's revolver. He'd taught her how to use a handgun, but she'd never had occasion to even consider using it to defend herself until now. Then, armed and frightened, she crept out into the hall.

Almost shaking too hard to aim, she opened the door across the hall that had once been Edward's suite, and as she had thought, the carpet was littered with shards of glass.

"Carley!" Hearing her name being called out startled her. As she tried to decide whether to run or shoot out the other window in hopes of scaring the intruder away, she heard her name called again from below the broken window.

Cautiously she crossed the room, her slippers crunching the broken glass, and peeped around the edge of the window. "Jordan!" she exclaimed as she recognized him. "What on earth do you think you're doing? You scared the hell out of me."

"I'm sorry. Come down and let me in."

"I'll do no such thing! What do you mean by breaking my window?"

"That was an accident. I threw a pebble, but you didn't hear it. I guess I threw too big a rock."

"This isn't my bedroom, anyway."

"It's not? Who can tell in a house like this? Come downstairs."

"I'm not going to do any such thing. Go away!"

"I won't leave until we talk."

"I don't want to talk to you. I want you to leave."

"Not until you tell me why you left."

Carley shoved open the unbroken window and leaned out. "Will you be quiet? The neighbors will hear you!"

"Your neighbors are all asleep."

"You don't know that."

"Why did you leave?"

"Jordan, get out of my yard!"

"Are you going to shoot me with that thing or throw it at me?"

When she realized she was gesturing with the gun, she tossed it onto the bed. "I ought to. Go away!"

"I'm not leaving until you answer my question."

A flashing of red and blue lights from down the street caught Carley's attention. She groaned. "Damn!"

Jordan turned as the lights got closer. "You called the police?"

"It's the burglar alarm system. I forgot about it. You set off the silent alarm when you broke the window."

"It's a good thing I'm not a real burglar or I'd be long gone by now. Especially with all those lights flashing."

As the police car slowed to turn in her drive, Carley said, "Run! Get out of here!"

"And be shot running from the scene? No way, lady. I'm a better lawyer than that."

Carley could have sunk gladly through the floor as Harley Adamson got out of the car. She had known Harley all her life. He had graduated from high school the year before Jordan and herself.

"Hold it right there!" Harley yelled as he saw Jordan in the strobe effect of his police lights.

"It's just me, Harley. Jordan Landry." Jordan's voice sounded as calm as if they were meeting on a street corner at midday.

"Jordan? Is that really you?" As Harley came nearer, he pushed his gun back in his holster. "What in the sam hill are you doing over here in the middle of the night?"

"I was just talking to Carley." Jordan looked up toward the window, and Carley shrank back.

She gathered her robe closer to her body and said with dignity, "It's a long story, Harley."

The policeman frowned at Jordan, then looked back up at Carley. "Is he giving you trouble? Looks like he was trying to break in."

Jordan sighed in exasperation. "Now, Harley, if I were trying to break in, don't you think I'd have sense enough to break a lower window?"

"I don't rightly know. You see just about everything on this job."

"I wanted to talk to Carley," Jordan explained with exaggerated patience. "I threw a rock to get her attention and the glass broke."

"Most folks use a telephone when they have talking in mind."

Carley wanted them both to leave. "I'm sorry to get you out here on a false call, Harley, but as you can see, there is no trouble. So if you two will be on your way..."

"I don't know," Harley said. "This sure looks peculiar. It's a wonder we haven't had calls from the neighbors complaining. I can't leave until you two cease and disperse."

"I can't cease because I'm not doing anything," she reasoned, "and I can't disperse because I live here. Disperse, Jordan."

"Carley, I have to talk to you!" Jordan insisted.

"You heard the lady," Harley said. "Go on home now."

"Not until I have a chance to talk to her. This is important."

The policeman tipped his hat back and said, "Jordan, I never knew you to be a drinking and carousing man. Don't make me haul you in for a breathalyzer test."

Jordan glared at him. "You can damn well tell I'm not drunk, Harley. I'm just put out at all this."

Harley shook his head. "All I see is a man standing where he don't belong in the middle of the night, a busted window and Carley in her nightgown."

Carley drew back farther. "I've had enough of this! I'm going back to bed. You two work it out between you, but don't bother me anymore."

She slammed the window so hard that the rest of the glass in the broken window tinkled onto the carpet. Angrily she stalked downstairs to turn off the alarm, then went back to her room, threw her robe onto a chair and jumped into bed. Throwing her forearm over her eyes, she tried not to shake with anger. Her life had been so much simpler before Jordan Landry had come back to town.

Early the next morning Carley called the Carstair Glass Company and had Charley Carstair come out to repair her window. She knew Shelley would have the news as soon as she talked to her husband, but Charley was the only glass repairman in town.

Minutes after Charley arrived, Arthur pulled into the drive and knocked imperiously on her door. "You're out early," she said cautiously as she let him into the house.

"I've already heard the news. It's all over town," he fumed.

"What is? Do you want some coffee?"

"No! Sarah Jean Adamson is telling everybody at the beauty shop that her husband had to come over here last night."

Carley turned and went back to the kitchen to pour herself another cup of coffee. "I had very little sleep last night and I'm not in the mood for a visit."

"I'm not here to visit, Carley!" Arthur paced the length of the kitchen and back. "Betsy heard it when Sarah Jean was shampooing her hair! Can you imagine the spot that put her in? She had to act as if nothing was wrong until after her hair was set and dried."

"That's not the end of the world, Arthur."

"Well? What really happened last night? To hear Sarah Jean's version, Harley had quite an eyeful!"

Carley paled. "What do you mean by that?"

"She said Jordan Landry was over here making a fuss and that you were in your nightgown!" He made the accusation sound scandalous.

"Oh, for heaven's sake! Jordan was in the yard, and I was talking to him from an upstairs window. You make it sound as if we were hosting an orgy."

"Sarah Jean made it sound that way, too!"

Carley burned her lips on the hot coffee. "When I get my hands on Harley Adamson, I'm going to pinch his head off! And Sarah Jean's, as well!"

"Obviously there was a bit more to it than a conversation. I saw Charley Carstair's truck out front."

"A window got broken. That's all that happened."

"It sounds pretty peculiar to me, Carley! I don't like having the McKay name linked to police reports!"

"I'm not thrilled by it either, Arthur!"

"And I don't want you to see Jordan again!"

Carley wheeled on him with a glare. She slammed her coffee cup down on the countertop, sloshing hot coffee everywhere. "You don't have the right to tell me what to do!"

"Somebody needs to!" he retorted.

"Get out of my house, Arthur! And don't you ever try to tell me whom I can or can't see, not ever again!"

Before Arthur could answer, there was a knock on the kitchen door. Fuming, Carley yanked open the door. Jordan was standing on her doorstep.

"Now we're going to talk," he said.

"Sure. Why not? Let's all talk." She waved him in and was gratified to see Arthur scowl. "If there's one thing I like doing first thing in the morning, it's talking."

"Jordan," Arthur said stiffly in greeting.

"Arthur," Jordan responded with a brief nod. They had never particularly liked each other.

Arthur said in his most pretentious voice, "I was just telling Carley that I think it would be better if you two break off your rather dubious friendship."

"I heard her reply as I came to the door. I agree with Carley. It's none of your business."

"I'm afraid it is my business when ugly rumors are circulating around town about my father's widow. It's my family name that's being besmirched."

"Besmirched?" Jordan said with a laugh. "Come off it, Arthur!"

"It seems," Carley said in cool tones, "that it's all over town about Harley coming out here last night and why."

"All you had to do was let me in, and there wouldn't have been a scene."

"Yes, there would. You had broken the window before I knew you were out there. The alarm had already gone off at the police station."

"Carley!" Arthur snapped. "You shouldn't tell everyone about our alarm system."

"I'm not a cat burglar," Jordan reminded him. "I usually enter a house by the door, not a window."

"Why didn't you ring the doorbell?" Carley asked. "I've been wondering about that."

"Your porch light was on, and I didn't want anyone to drive by and see me there at that time of night. I thought it might cause gossip. It never occurred to me that your windows were booby-trapped."

"An alarm system that cost what this one did," Arthur proclaimed, "is hardly in the class of booby trap."

Jordan ignored him. "I had to do some fast talking to keep Harley from taking me down to the police station. That was pretty rotten of you to leave me alone with him."

Carley shrugged and went back to her coffee cup.

"In view of everything, I think it's rotten of you to come back over here," Arthur said. "A man with any sensitivity at all would be able to reason that the lady doesn't want to see him."

"Go home, Arthur," Jordan said. "I have to talk to Carley in private."

"You have no right to order me to leave!"

"I do," Carley said, "and I want both of you to go."

"I'm not leaving," Jordan said, as he helped himself to a cup of coffee. "Not until I get an answer to the question I asked you last night. If you prefer to discuss it in front of Arthur, that's up to you."

Carley grabbed Arthur's elbow and pulled him toward the door. He had no choice but to go. As he left, he glared at them both.

"There! See what you've done?" she exclaimed. "Now he'll go straight to Betsy, and they'll talk all morning about what that question might be!"

"So?"

"I don't enjoy being the subject of speculation. Especially not theirs." She came back and stared out the kitchen window. "I can't believe any of this! When other women date, it's not on the five o'clock news."

Jordan laughed as he hoisted himself up to sit on the countertop. "Why did you leave last night?"

"Abby would wonder if I came dragging in this morning."

"That's it? You didn't want to shock your maid?" He looked at her incredulously. "Where is she?"

"Shopping for groceries. And probably hearing all about last night from the check-out girl. I hate for people to talk about me, and it's all over town."

"I don't believe Abby is the only reason you left. There are ways to get around inquisitive maids."

She looked up in curiosity but was too proud to ask what he'd meant.

"What's the rest of it?"

"It's because I don't want to just have an affair. I need more than that."

Jordan frowned. "I thought we *had* more than that."

"No, we don't. Sex isn't reason enough for two people to go to bed with each other."

"Well, you have to admit it was damned good sex." She glared at him.

"Carley, I've told you I don't want to get married. I don't want to constantly be around someone making demands and whining when she doesn't get her way."

"I never whine!"

"I don't want a long-term commitment."

"Then you don't want me!" she retorted.

"Unfortunately, I do. And I don't know what in the hell to do about it. Can't you simply enjoy what we have for as long as it lasts?"

"No."

"Carley, I know people whose affairs have lasted for years!"

"According to a magazine article I read, the average is six weeks."

"Well, it could be a fine six weeks. One you could think back on for the rest of your life."

She turned her angry eyes on him. "Forget it. I want more around me in my old age than memories."

"You beat everything. You know that? You look and sound like a modern woman, but your thinking is Victorian."

"Morals and standards are important to me!"

"They are to me, too, but I'm not fanatic over them!"

"You think I'm a fanatic? Get out of my kitchen!"

Jordan drew in a steadying breath. "No, I don't think you're a fanatic. I'm not sure what I think you are. It's just that you can make me mad easier than anyone else in town. You're exasperating."

"Only to you. Everyone else seems to like me well enough."

"I like you, too. That's the problem. If I didn't, I'd know what to do about you."

She studied him carefully, then said, "I like you, too."

"You don't have to make it sound as if you're pulling teeth to say it."

"You did. I could say the same thing about you."

"So where do you want to go from here?"

"I don't know. I really don't know."

"I don't want you running away in the middle of the night. I was worried sick about you."

"You were? I never thought of that." She lowered her eyes in embarrassment. "I've never... I had never been in that predicament before, and I didn't know how to handle it. I didn't know if I was supposed to wake you up or what." She lifted her chin defiantly. "I don't know how to have an affair."

He smiled and reached out to touch her cheek. "We could figure it out as we go along."

"Jordan!"

"Well, there aren't any hard and fast rules, as far as I know. It's giving and taking just like any other relationship. Only closer."

Carley sighed. Why, of all the people in the world, did she have to fall in love with him? Not once, but twice! She should have her head examined.

"Well? Will you see me again?"

She nodded. "But I can't guarantee I'll be more than your friend."

"That's good enough. For now."

She looked up at him and found him smiling at her with the look she'd come to know was uniquely meant for her. It was that look that always robbed her of her willpower. A movement in the drive drew her attention. "Abby is back. If she finds you sitting on her countertop, she'll run you through the blender."

Jordan vaulted down and kissed her lightly. "Will you come over for supper tonight? I'll put some steaks on the grill." When she hesitated, he added, "And we can practice our lines."

Carley nodded. That gave her conscience an excuse. "I guess so."

"Come over about seven. That way you have your car handy in case you want to make an escape." He winked at her and left before Abby could come in the house.

Carley sighed and tried to get her mind on her day's activities.

Chapter Twelve

Carley felt nervous as she drove into Jordan's driveway and parked. All day she had been able to think of nothing but him. Dozens of times she had mentally reconstructed their conversations and his smile and the way he moved and talked. And especially the way they had made love.

Jordan came around the house to meet her, wearing a red shirt and jeans that hugged his slim hips and muscular thighs. She thought he was as handsome as a movie idol.

"I've started the charcoal. We can put the steaks on in a little while. Would you like some wine?"

"Yes, I would. Thanks." Obviously, she thought, all the nervousness about their off-again, on-again relationship was on her side. Jordan never seemed discomforted about anything.

"I like that dress," he was saying as he escorted her around to the side of the house. "You look as cool as a tall glass of frosty lemonade."

She smiled. She had given her looks a lot of consideration, and the white eyelet sundress she'd chosen was a new one. But even with the lightweight dress and her hair piled up off her neck, she was still far from cool. "I've never seen such a hot summer."

"It won't be long before fall will be here. At least we got some rain. Dry weather is too hard on the farmers and ranchers. I've had a lot of clients fighting foreclosures."

"They say a hard summer means a severe winter," she said. "Personally I don't care as long as we get some relief from this heat."

Jordan held open the door to his screened-in side porch for Carley to enter, then he followed her in. The breeze from a ceiling fan brought welcome relief. "How was your day?" he asked.

Carley glanced at him, wondering if he knew how homey that question had sounded. "Fine. And yours?"

"Busy. Everybody wants to sue everybody else. I think it's a combination of the heat and a full moon. At least Apple Tree isn't prone to violent crimes. This is the time of year they are most prevalent."

"Is that true? I never heard that."

"I swear."

She was quiet for a minute as he poured them each a glass of Chablis he'd been chilling in the small refrigerator on the porch. "Starting tomorrow we rehearse every night. Now the grind begins."

"True, but I'm looking forward to it." He grinned. "With nightly rehearsals, I know I'll see you at least once each day."

"My social calendar isn't all that jammed. You could see me every day, anyway."

He sat beside her on the blue and white cushions of the rattan couch. "I've been thinking about that quite a bit today. Seeing you daily, that is. I like the idea."

"Oh?"

"You're addictive."

"That sounds like the C word to me."

"Commitment? I don't know. I really don't. Until I came back to Apple Tree, I was so sure what I wanted— and what I didn't want—out of life. Now I just don't know."

Carley smiled and sipped her wine. Like herself, Jordan was a product of Apple Tree and, whether he espoused loose morals or not, she had a feeling his traditional upbringing wasn't completely erased.

He put the steaks on the grill while Carley finished making the salad, and when the meat was done to order, they ate in the cool shade of the porch. She loved the companionable silences, and delighted that they frequently broke that silence by both starting to talk at the same time. They laughed and talked about noncontroversial things, and for the first time since his return, they shared a relaxing time together. Carley didn't know when her nervousness had left but was glad it had gone.

"If only it could be like this between us all the time," she said with a contented sigh as they settled back onto the couch. "No arguments, no difficult decisions. This is great."

"It could be, if you'll agree to always let me have my way," he teased.

Carley laughed. "Or if you always let me have mine. And if you didn't put any pressure on me."

"I never use pressure. I coerce."

"I can recognize pressure when I see it. Besides, it's much too hot to argue."

"Would you rather go inside where it's cooler?"

She shook her head. "It's almost sunset. This is my favorite time of day."

"I'll carry our plates to the kitchen, and we'll walk down to watch the sun set over the lake. It's prettier there."

"I'll help you."

"No, you're to sit here and stay happy. I'll be right back."

Carley watched him go into the house. He was so wonderful, she thought lovingly. Jordan embodied every trait she had ever wanted in a man. Plus a few like stubbornness and teasing that she could do with less of. But his perverseness made him human, she decided. Otherwise he would be too good to be true.

The phone rang, interrupting her reverie. Carley leaned forward. "Jordan? Should I get that?" When there was no answer, she went in the door and picked up the receiver. "Hello?"

There was a pause, and a voice she knew quite well said, "Is Jordan there?"

"Of course. Just a minute." Carley gripped the phone. Melissa had given no sign that she recognized Carley's voice, though Carley felt she must have. She went into the kitchen where Jordan was running water over the plates. "There's a phone call for you."

"Oh? I didn't hear it ring."

"I think it's Melissa."

Jordan looked displeased. "I'd better take it in the den. Will you hang up the extension, please?"

"Of course." She felt suddenly awkward, as if she were an intruder.

Jordan quickly crossed the kitchen and went into the den. Carley listened for him to pick up the receiver, then hung up. Her fingers lingered for a minute on the phone. Why was Melissa calling Jordan?

Jordan cradled the receiver between his jaw and shoulder. "Hello?"

"This is Melissa. I'm sorry to bother you. That was Carley, wasn't it?"

"Yes, it was. What's up?"

She drew a wavering breath. "Jack was over here."

"Damn!" Jordan dropped into his chair, tightening his grip on the phone. "What happened? Are you okay?"

"Yes. Just scared. He called this afternoon and threatened me again. I told him you had a peace bond against him and that he would be put in jail if he didn't leave me alone."

"What did he say to that?"

"He just laughed and said peace bonds don't mean a thing."

"Unfortunately he's right. They're more of a threat than anything."

"He hung up, and when I looked out the window a few minutes later, he was standing there."

"In the yard?"

"No, you know how my yard stops a few feet past the driveway by that side road? He was on the other side of the road under that maple tree, just standing there staring at the window. He just kept standing there and staring." Melissa's voice quavered as if she was on the verge of tears.

"Has Jack gone now?"

"Yes, finally. I left the room to start supper, and a minute later I looked back out and he was gone. I didn't see him leave. Jordan, it was so eerie!"

"Okay, calm down. Are all your doors and windows locked?"

"Yes. Yes, I checked them first thing. What if he comes back?"

"If he does, call the police first, then me. I'm going to call and tell them to get out there fast if you call."

"Thank you. I'm so sorry to bother you, but I didn't know what else to do."

"It's no problem. Carley came over for dinner and to rehearse our lines, so we'll be here."

"You won't tell her why I called, will you? I don't want anyone to know."

"Of course I won't. This is strictly confidential."

"Thank you so much. Carley is my friend but, well, it's just embarrassing."

"Don't worry about it. Go eat your supper and get your mind off your troubles. In a few days your divorce will be final and you can get on with your new life."

"You've been such a help to me. I really appreciate it."

Jordan said goodbye, then hung up. He dialed the number of the police station, identified himself and told them what had happened and that he suspected Jack Thompson might violate his peace bond. He asked that any calls for help from his client, Melissa Thompson, be taken very seriously and be responded to immediately. He wasn't sure his call would make the police act with any more efficiency, but a reminder that an attorney would be monitoring their performance couldn't hurt.

When he returned to the screened-in porch, Carley was looking out at the soft evening colors and didn't turn to acknowledge him. "Would you like to walk down to the lake?"

When she continued staring out across the lawn in silence, he guessed she was troubled that Melissa had called. He couldn't explain, however, because he had given his word. He waited patiently for her to make the next move.

A few moments later, she said, "I'd like that."

Awkwardly holding hands, they walked across the lawn and around to the back of the house. As Carley's gaze swept the expanse of the lake, its surface returning the colors of the setting sun, her attention stopped on the structure Jordan had been working on. When she caught her breath, she exclaimed, "A gazebo!"

"I just finished it."

"You built it? Why didn't you tell me?"

He looked at her curiously. He had never thought she would be interested.

Carley hurried to it and caressed one of the satiny white uprights that supported the gingerbread-laced roof. "All my life I've pictured myself in a house with a gazebo out back. Don't you remember? I told you about it time and time again. We even said we would have one someday." She realized what she was saying and fell silent.

Jordan suddenly remembered. A gazebo *had* featured in the future Carley had fantasized for them. On a conscious level he had forgotten it, but a part of him must have remembered. Why else would he have built one? Had he been picturing Carley in it all along? As his wife? "I don't know what to say."

She smiled shyly. "You don't need to say anything. It's beautiful. I never knew you had any carpenter skills."

"Don't you remember? I used to work with Dad every summer." He studied the gazebo. Why had he built it?

"I'd forgotten," Carley said as she went up the shallow steps and across the octagonal deck. "How lovely! Look, Jordan, the sun is going down. What wonderful colors!"

His face was a mask as he stared up at the gazebo's roof, but his mind puzzled over this enigma. Carley as his wife? He didn't want a wife.

"That strip of gold cloud looks like a finger stretching across the sun." When she heard no response, she glanced back at him. "Jordan?"

"Right," he said quickly. "It sure does."

"Is something wrong?"

"Nope. Not a thing." Carley as his wife. If he wanted anyone for a wife, it would be Carley. No! He enjoyed his freedom, and the gazebo didn't mean a thing.

With deep breaths Carley inhaled the clean air. "Evening smells so sweet. Like all the flowers are blooming."

"It's the roses and honeysuckle," he said. "Once the air starts to cool, their fragrance seems to get stronger." He took a deep breath. "And four o'clocks. Over there. See?"

She looked at the masses of pink, white and yellow blossoms on the nearby hedge. "All the scents of our childhood. Remember how we used to suck the honey taste out of honeysuckle blooms?"

"And pop rose petals to see who could make the loudest sound?"

"And the time your Uncle Ned set the garage on fire because he was trying to get rid of the four o'clocks your aunt had planted next to it?"

Jordan laughed. "Aunt Grace gave him hell over that."

Their eyes met, and their laughter faded away. For a long moment neither spoke, and Carley's pulse quickened in her throat. Hastily she looked away. "It looks as if the water is on fire," she said. "I don't think I've ever seen such a glorious sunset."

"It's the dust in the air," he said absently. "We need more rain."

Hesitantly she turned back to him. She wanted him to admit that he'd built the gazebo because he knew how much it would mean to her. But then that might not have been the reason. She was afraid to ask him.

Jordan stepped up behind her and cradled her against his chest so they could watch the sunset together. "This is the time of day I'm always the loneliest," he confided.

Her throat felt constricted. "For Cindy Lou?"

"No," he said with a short laugh. "No, I miss Kevin."

"You rarely talk about him."

"It hurts too much."

She nodded and felt his chin against her hair. "This is family time. Everybody is coming home from work or play and getting ready to sit down together at the table. Sunset and Sundays are the hardest."

"And holidays," he added.

"And holidays," she agreed.

"Do you miss Edward as much as you said you do?"

Carley thought for a minute. "I'm not sure anymore. I did, but now... it's as if he was part of another
life. One that's not a part of me any longer."

She felt the warmth of his breath and a tingle as he
kissed her ear, then her neck. "I'm not the same person now."

"I'm not sure you ever were," he said softly. "Not
really."

"Maybe not." She wanted him to continue kissing
her like that forever. Her entire body was suddenly
warm and pliable. "I know I was the one who had to do
all the changing."

"You're exactly the way I like you." His lips brushed
the shell of her ear, and he nuzzled the loose tendrils at
the back of her neck.

"Am I?"

He turned her to face him and gathered her into his
arms. "When I first saw you on that stage, I was
stunned," he said softly. "You were the same, and yet
you weren't the same at all. You had the sparkle I remembered, but you've added a maturity."

Her breath seemed to be caught in her throat. "I
guess that came from learning to dance in heels," she
managed to say.

"And you had gone from pretty girl to beautiful
woman. Where did the freckles go that I loved to kiss?"
He kissed her nose and cheeks where they had been.

"If I spend any time in the sun, you'll see them
again."

"I wouldn't change anything about you. Stay with me
tonight, Carley. *All* night."

"I shouldn't." Her voice was soft because his kisses
were stealing her strength.

"But will you?"

Slowly she nodded, her cheek pressed against his. "I want to stay."

"All night?"

She smiled mischievously. "I have to. My reputation can't afford any more broken windows."

"Your mother always did predict I'd grow up to be a hoodlum."

"Mom was wrong about several things."

He gazed down into her eyes, and she felt as if her blood had turned to molten lava. He had a way of turning the most trivial conversation into a sensual invitation.

"Why do you want me to spend the night?" she asked.

"I want to sleep beside you and have your warm body wake me up. I want to make love to you off and on all night, and to find you beside me when the sun comes up."

She smiled. "I'd like that. But what if you don't like the way I look in the morning?"

He grinned his sexiest grin even before he spoke. "I've seen you in the morning, and you're beautiful. I want time to enjoy you and please you without Arthur ringing the doorbell or Abby coming in to clean. We can have privacy here; you live in a fishbowl."

"I like it here." She looked up the rising lawn to the Victorian house the sunset had transformed into a pink and gold confection. "You live in a fairy-tale house. That's the way I've always thought of this place. And now it even has a gazebo."

He led her to the rattan couch, and they sat on the plump cushions. "I'm glad I built it. Look at that view."

"That's something else I like about you," she said as she slipped into his embrace. "You're not in a hurry. I've agreed to spend the night, and you aren't dragging me up the hill to throw me on your bed."

His silver eyes met hers. "I have all night. You'll be in my bed in time."

"Heaven help me," she said with a sigh, "but I do care about you."

"I care about you, too." His eyes told her this was an understatement. His eyes held love.

Carley lifted her face to his and drew him down to her kiss. His lips were soft and warm, his kiss filled with provocative promises. She wondered what she would do if he didn't love her. She wasn't sure she could have survived having him leave her again. Surely he loved her! How could he kiss her with such ardor and look at her with so much desire unless he loved her? And he had built the gazebo. That had to mean something; no one built a gazebo by accident.

Jordan ran his hand up the silky skin of her thigh. Because of the heat Carley had worn neither hose nor bra. Now she wondered if she had left them off with this in mind. He slid his fingers under the elastic of her panties and stroked her with loving tenderness. Carley's body quickened at once.

"You're so responsive," he murmured. "I feel as if you're somehow programmed for my touch."

She smiled because it was true. No one but Jordan had ever evoked an immediate response in her, or had given her loving that brought a series of heart-stopping climaxes. "You're special," she whispered. "So very special."

He ran his hand back down her thigh and over the crisp eyelet of her dress to caress her slender waist. Then he stroked higher, letting his thumb follow the outer swell of her breast. Slowly he drew his fingers over the curves of her shoulder and around her neck to trace down to the cleavage above her bodice. Moving with sensual deliberation, Jordan released first one pearl button, then the next.

"Out here?" she asked in surprise.

"No one will see us. We're hidden from the road, and I have no close neighbors."

She glanced around, and for the first time noticed they were indeed secluded. The sun had gone down behind the distant trees, leaving behind shadows of purple and blue. A full moon was rising on the other side of the lake, but its beams had not yet reached the gazebo. "I've never made love outside."

"No? Neither have I."

"You haven't?"

"Big-city life doesn't lend itself to that sort of thing. Nights in Apple Tree are much more pleasant and private."

He opened the other buttons and brushed the fabric away, revealing the fullness of her breasts. In the pale light they were as luminous as pearl, and her pouting nipples were a dusky rose. "Beautiful!" he said reverently. "You're so beautiful."

When his hard palm covered one of her breasts, Carley's nipples beaded tighter. Her flesh mounded under his hand, and her desire began to build. He rubbed his palm over her nipple, then teased it with his fingers until she moved restlessly with desire. Her love for him raced with her passion, and she had to catch her lip between her teeth not to speak of her love.

Jordan replaced his fingers with his lips and sucked gently as his hands found their way under her full skirt.

Carley followed his urging and stood in front of him, her dress about her hips and her eyes sultry with invitation. With her eyes on his, she reached up and removed the pins from her hair, one by one, and put them into his shirt pocket. When her hair was loose, she shook her head, and her auburn tresses tumbled down about her bare shoulders.

Then she stepped out of her sandals and found the smooth deck of the gazebo was cool under her feet. Gradually she unbuttoned his shirt and pulled it off.

"You're one sexy lady," Jordan observed in a husky voice.

"You inspire me." It was true. She would never have wanted to sexually tease anyone else. She never had.

As Jordan watched, she reached up under her skirt and pulled off her panties, then dropped the bit of white lace on his scarlet shirt.

Jordan unzipped his jeans and removed the rest of his clothes as she smiled and let him look at her moonwashed breasts. Before he could take the lead, she gently pushed him back down onto the couch and straddled his lap, facing him.

She put her arms around him and kissed him with all the passion in her soul. Of all the men in the world, this was the one she wanted, and she was going to show him her love even if she didn't dare speak it.

The position Carley had assumed left both Jordan's hands free to toy with her breasts. Carley felt her desire increase as he enjoyed and pleasured her. When he moaned softly from wanting her, she shifted slightly and took him into her body.

For a minute she was still as she relished the hot sensation of their oneness. Then she began to rock back and forth.

Jordan pushed aside her skirt and slipped his hand between their bodies. His thumb found the seat of her desire, and Carley murmured with pleasure as he stroked it.

As ecstasy grew, she moved faster, feeling the incredible pleasure intensify until she could hold back no longer. As she reached her completion, she felt Jordan clasp her tightly and knew hers had triggered his own.

"I couldn't hold back," he said as if the fact surprised him. "I wanted you so much, and it felt so damned good, I just couldn't hold back."

Carley smiled at him smugly. "We have all night."

Chapter Thirteen

Are you going to sleep all day?"

Carley opened her eyes and inhaled the delicious aroma of toast and coffee. "What time is it?" she asked with a satisfied smile.

"Late. Nearly six-thirty."

"In the morning?" She fell back with a groan on the pillow. "Don't you *ever* sleep?"

"I have something else in mind."

Carley opened her eyes again. "Oh?" Her smile broadened.

"Take a bite." Jordan fed her some toast smeared with butter and strawberry jam, then took a bite himself. "I didn't know if you take your coffee black, so I brought it all."

"Good. I put everything I can find in it."

"Sissy. Open your mouth."

Carley let him feed her while she added cream and sugar to her coffee. "I think I'm beginning to wake up now. Why, you brought me a rose!"

"Fresh from the garden."

She breathed in the flower's fragrance, then held it under Jordan's nose. "I love roses. Especially pink ones like this. They smell sweeter than red ones."

"You're a sensuous lady. I never noticed there was a difference."

"It hasn't impaired your sensuality," she said with a smile.

Jordan let her finish her coffee, then whisked away the tray. "Get dressed. We're going for a canoe ride."

"This early in the morning?"

"It's the only time. A couple of hours from now it will be too hot. I put a pair of Aunt Estelle's shorts and one of my T-shirts on that chair. The canoe might prove to be an undoing for your dress."

Although she was a bit reticent for such an early morning adventure, she wanted nothing more than to please Jordan, so she hastily dressed in one of Jordan's shirts and a pair of his aunt's shorts. While she and Jordan's aunt were about the same height, their girths and taste in clothes were somewhat different. Luckily Jordan's T-shirt covered the short's loose waist and wild, flowered pattern.

"Perfect," he proclaimed. "You should wear hand-me-downs all the time."

"You have such a way with words."

Jordan put on a pair of faded cutoffs and a T-shirt that might once have been red. Across the front was the name of a baseball team and on the back was a number six. "Leave your shoes here," he advised. "They might get wet."

"Are you sure this is going to be fun? You're wearing tennis shoes. What if I step on a grass burr?"

"I've thought of that," he said as they went downstairs. As they stepped onto the porch, he swooped her up in his arms. "I'll carry you."

"Jordan!" She laughed with pretended alarm. "Put me down!"

"Quit squirming or I'll drop you."

She knew he wouldn't, but she relaxed in his arms. "If I had known how gallant you were going to be, I wouldn't have eaten so much toast."

"No problem, ma'am. I can carry you, toast and all."

When they reached the edge of the lake, Jordan put her down on the narrow ribbon of sand. With a practiced motion he flipped the overturned canoe into the water. He held out his hand to her as he steadied the boat. "Careful. The bottom of the lake drops off pretty sharply here."

Carley edged into the water, laughing as the cool waves lapped about her ankles and the firm sand oozed between her toes. He was right about the bottom sloping, and she was glad to have his firm hand to steady her. She stepped into the canoe and sat on the seat he'd indicated.

As Jordan joined her, the canoe rocked precariously until he was seated. Once he was settled, he took a paddle from the brackets beside the seats and sent the boat out over the water in a gliding sweep.

Carley laughed as they tried to make their way through the verses of "Red Wing," the only song about Indians either of them could remember.

The sun was barely up, and the air was still soft from the night. A cool breeze stroked across the lake, and the bordering willow trees nodded in approval. A cow in the meadow opposite the lake lifted her head and chewed grass solemnly before deciding to ignore them.

"It's a good thing Bob didn't hear your rendition of 'Red Wing' before casting you," she teased. She had laughed so much that her sides were aching.

"You've wounded me to the quick. So 'Red Wing' isn't classy enough? How about this?" He burst into "Some Enchanted Evening," his powerful voice booming over the water.

"Enough, enough!" she shouted with a laugh. "You're scaring the cow."

Jordan laughed as he watched the lazy animal chewing methodically. "She doesn't look too scared to me."

"She's putting on a show of bravery. She's petrified. I'll bet she doesn't give milk for days."

"I'll bet she doesn't, either. Herefords are beef cattle." He poked her teasingly. "How did you grow up in the country and not learn any more than that about farm animals?"

"I had other priorities," she said with a parody of haughtiness. "*I* can dance in heels."

Jordan joined in her laughter as he paddled them in a long curve around the lake.

Carley had never been so happy. After spending the entire night in Jordan's arms, she was too much in love for her feet to touch the ground. He was an inventive as well as tender lover, and she felt as if her soul were singing. She had never been served breakfast in bed, much less with a rose, nor had she greeted the dawn in a canoe. She felt breathlessly young, vibrant and alive. All her worries were mirages. Only her love for Jordan was real.

She did love him. She loved him with an intensity as well as a bubbling joy and a soaring passion. Several times during the night she had been sure he was about to tell her that he loved her. She was positive he was going to ask her to marry him. She knew what her answer would be—yes! A glorious, soul-singing yes.

"What are you thinking about?" he asked. "You look like the cat that ate the canary."

Carley laughed and lifted her face to the cool breeze. "I was thinking about last night."

With a satisfied smile, Jordan took them on to the end of the lake where tall willows trailed their lithe branches into the water. A beetle as black as a jet bead left an ever-widening wake as he swam across the still water. A few golden willow leaves floated on the surface. Beyond the bank, the woods had been cleared of underbrush, leaving the area almost parklike.

"How beautiful!"

"I mow it. Otherwise you couldn't see the ground for haw bushes and weeds. Someday I may put a picnic table here. It's a ways from the house, but it's not a bad walk."

"You could get horses, and we could ride over."

Jordan paused a moment as if taken aback, then said, "Yes, I could get horses."

She realized too late that she had included herself in plans for his future. Until he proposed, she had no right to intimate such things. "I mean, you have that little barn. I guess it has a stall or two."

"It does. You know, a couple of horses might be a good idea. I've always enjoyed horseback riding."

Carley smiled. He knew she did, too. Most of her childhood had been spent on a horse.

"I'll look into that," he said decisively. "After the play is over. Starting tonight we will be there whenever we aren't working or sleeping."

"Speaking of work, aren't you going to be late?"

"My first appointment isn't until nine. I'm doing my best to keep city hours in the morning and country hours at closing time."

"You never were a candidate to become a workaholic."

"No need to be at the rates I charge," he said with a grin.

"We never did go over our lines," she reminded him.

"I know. That was just a clever ruse to lure you over here."

"I have to hand it to you. It worked great."

"Thanks. I'll try it again sometime."

Carley smiled. Was he teasing her? She had assumed she would be here on a fairly regular basis in view of the loving they had shared.

Jordan turned the canoe toward the gazebo and lustily launched into their duet. On cue Carley joined her voice to his as they skimmed across the still waters.

"We sound pretty good out here," he said. "Maybe we should talk Bob into turning *Moonbeams and Roses* into a water ballet."

"I'll let you be the one to suggest it to Chester," Carley said. "He goes into a decline every time someone misses so much as a word."

"I'll bet he has an ulcer," Jordan said.

"He should. He's earned it."

The canoe nosed up to the bank a couple of feet down from where they had boarded. "Carley, wait—"

But his words came too late. Carley had swung her leg over the side and was going into the water as she was saying, "I'll steady it and—" She slipped completely underwater and came up sputtering.

Jordan tried not to laugh, but a snicker escaped as he said, "I was about to say, let me paddle closer to the beach sand. It's still too deep here."

"Give me your hand," she said, pretending to be miffed.

He was laughing in earnest as he reached down to help her out. Carley waited until he was off balance, then braced her foot on the canoe and pulled. Jordan tumbled over the side and landed with a giant splash. With a shriek she swam frantically for the beach, hoping to outdistance him. But Jordan was too fast for her, and soon she felt his fingers close around her ankle. As he pulled back on her, his head slid under the water. Carley turned back and pushed his shoulder farther under the surface.

Laughing they both surfaced. Grazing the sand with her toes, Carley stroked backward until she could stand chin deep in the water. "Why, Jordan," she said innocently, "you're all wet."

He swam to her and ducked her again before he headed back out to retrieve the drifting canoe.

Carley shook her head, sending a shower of lake water from her hair as Jordan pulled the canoe up onto the grass and upended it. "I guess I'll wash my hair today," she commented.

"Might as well. It's already wet." His eyes traveled down the wet T-shirt that was clinging to her as closely as a second skin. "I never thought that shirt could look so good."

Carley glanced down and saw the clearly defined pucker of her nipples. She pulled the cloth away, but it settled back, emphasizing her breasts.

"Yep, that shirt is going to be one of my favorites from now on," Jordan confirmed.

Carley grinned. "Just how long is it until your nine o'clock appointment?"

"We have plenty of time if we hurry." He picked her up and ran with her toward the house.

As she closed the door behind her, the phone rang.

"Damn!" He glared at the phone as if it were an intruder.

"You'd better put me down and answer it."

With a disgruntled sigh Jordan lowered her bare feet to the floor and reached for the receiver. "Hello?"

Carley went to the downstairs bathroom to get towels to dry themselves with. As she returned she heard him say, "What's up, Melissa?"

She froze in place, a cold fist knotting inside her. She might love Jordan and she might want him to love her, but he still hadn't said he loved her. And he obviously had a life apart from her—one that clearly involved Melissa. She stepped back into the kitchen and held out the towel.

Jordan took it and tried to hide his feeling of discomfort. Holding his palm over the mouthpiece, he said, "Will you excuse me a minute?"

"Sure."

He thought Carley's voice sounded a bit too forced, but he couldn't do anything about that now. Not when Melissa was crying hysterically on the other end. As soon as Carley left the room, he closed the door and said, "Jack did what?"

"He...he painted words—awful words—all over my house. Oh, God, Jordan, he says he will kill me before he lets me divorce him!"

"Did you call the police?"

"Yes, but they said they couldn't do anything because no one saw him do it. Jordan, they're *awful* words. The police say it's just vandalism, and they say they can't arrest Jack for it without proof.''

Jordan scowled. If no one saw Jack in the act, there was no case against him. He glanced at the kitchen clock. ''I have an appointment in an hour, but I can come over then.'' He looked up to see that Carley had come in the other doorway. She was dressed and had towel dried her hair. ''Hang on a minute, Melissa.''

Carley lifted her chin imperiously. ''I have to go now. It's later than I thought. Goodbye.''

''Wait a minute!'' Jordan spoke back into the receiver. ''Hang on, Melissa. Don't hang up.'' He dropped the phone onto the counter and hurried after Carley. ''Wait, Carley! Where are you going?''

''Home. I heard you making a date with Melissa.'' She hissed the words out in a whisper so Melissa couldn't overhear. ''When I agreed to come over, I didn't know I would have to take a number and get back in line if I went beyond my allotted time.'' Her dark eyes snapped with anger.

''Dammit, it's not like that!''

''No? Then explain it to me.'' She cocked her head to one side and crossed her arms beneath her breasts.

Jordan glared down at her. He couldn't explain without jeopardizing the confidentiality of a client. Besides, he thought Carley should trust him implicitly. ''I can't explain.''

''I thought not.'' Carley turned to go.

Jordan caught her arm. ''Don't go like this. You just have to trust me.''

''Do I? I don't think so. I trusted you before, and you married Cindy Lou. Who will it be this time? Melissa?''

''Don't do this, Carley!''

"You have no right to tell me what to do! Melissa evidently calls here constantly, and I heard you making a date with her!"

"I'm not making a date! It's business!"

"Business?"

"That's right. And I can't tell you any more than that because it *is* business and it's confidential."

Carley's eyes wavered. "Are you telling me the truth?"

"Yes, of course I am."

"It's just business?"

"That's right." He kissed her quickly. "I have to get back on the phone. Are you all right?"

"Yes," she said in a softer voice. "I'm sorry, Jordan. I thought . . ."

"I know. But you have to trust me, Carley."

She smiled uncertainly. "I will. I'm embarrassed, but I thought . . ."

"It's okay. Just forget about it. Will you come over tonight after rehearsal?"

Her smile broadened. "I'd love to."

He winked at her. "Go home and get some rest. Get plenty of rest."

She was laughing and feeling terribly foolish as she let herself out.

Stacy was curled in the overstuffed chair in Carley's bedroom watching her friend assemble her costume. "So you've started dating Jordan? I'm so glad."

Carley's eyes held stars as she said, "He's wonderful. So exciting and intelligent, and he has a sense of humor. He's wonderful!"

"Does this mean you may be something more meaningful to each other than friends, as Chester would put it?"

With a blush Carley put her blue shirtwaist on the bed with her slip and box of navy pumps. "We're just dating, Stacy. Don't read any more into it than that. I don't want any more gossip to start."

"I wasn't planning to put it in the paper." Stacy paused. "Is he seeing anyone else? Socially, I mean?"

"Nope. Just me. Hand me that hairbrush."

Stacy got the brush for her, and Carley began to pack her makeup bag. She rummaged through her dresser drawer in search of the sticks of cream stage makeup and blushers.

"Bill said he saw Jordan's car over at Melissa's the other day."

Carley nodded. "She's his client, you know. Where could I have put that highlighter stick? I should have started gathering up this stuff last week."

"I have some in the prop room that you can borrow." She added, "Melissa says her divorce will be final in a couple of days."

"That's right." She unearthed a plastic container. "Finally! Now where is my red liner?"

"I guess I'm just worried needlessly," Stacy said. "After all you've told me about the way Jordan treated you in the past, I'm afraid you'll get hurt again."

"So was I," Carley admitted, "but Jordan says I have to trust him."

"When did he say that?"

"This morning, when he was talking to Melissa. Don't look so concerned. It was a business call. He told me so."

Stacy nodded but didn't answer.

Carley found the red liner she used to add sparkle to her eyes and tossed it into the bag. "What about that navy straw purse? Does it look like something Alice would carry?"

"Looks good to me. What about one of these flowers for your hair? Alice strikes me as a daisy-type person."

"Toss it in. I'll ask Bob."

"So Jordan was talking to Melissa this morning? And you were there?"

Carley nodded happily. "He asked me over again after rehearsal, too."

"Oh? Why doesn't he come over here?"

"You sound like my mother," Carley said with a laugh. "In the first act I think I'll wear my red skirt. Do you think my red-and-white sweater will be too hot?"

"Under those new lights? You'll fry. Wear the silk blouse you wore to Shelley's last luncheon."

Carley began assembling the outfit. "Thank goodness this isn't a period piece. No hoop skirts or trailing trains to worry about."

"That makes it easier on me, too, in the prop room. Have you ever tried to build a suit of armor?"

"He doesn't like to come over here because of Abby and Arthur being in and out all the time."

"Oh?"

Carley ignored her. "Which shoes go best with the red outfit?"

"The white ones."

Carley put the shoes in a box and put it on the bed. "Now for act two. I'm going to need a moving van to carry all this to the theater."

"Wear the camel skirt and jacket," Stacy suggested.

"For a girl right out of school? I think it's too sophisticated. How about this yellow sundress?"

"Perfect. And wear the sandals you have on. Do you need a purse with it?"

Carley studied her list of accessories. "No, Alice stays inside during this act."

"Carley, be careful."

"What?" She looked at Stacy in surprise. "Careful about what?"

"You know—Jordan. I can't help but remember how worried you were that he would hurt Melissa."

Carley sat on the bed and leaned forward toward her friend. "Don't worry about me. I'm a big girl now and not as naive by a long shot as I used to be. I have to trust Jordan or I can't have any meaningful relationship with him at all. You told me he had probably changed, remember? Well, you were right. He's wonderful, Stacy. Jordan is everything I've ever dreamed of."

"Are you in love with him?" Stacy exclaimed.

Shyly Carley nodded as she blushed. "But he doesn't know yet. I may tell him tonight."

"Then he also loves you?"

"I'm sure he does. Oh, Stacy, do you know what we did this morning? We went for a canoe ride and sang 'Red Wing.'"

"Sounds like the real thing to me," Stacy said with no conviction.

"It is, it really is!"

"If it's not, he had better look out for me. I don't want you to get hurt."

"Stacy, Stacy. You're such a worrier! If you want something to stew over, worry about how I can make the last scene believable. That's the one where Alice tells Buck she's leaving him and never wants to see him again. Now that's going to take some acting!"

Rehearsal went smoothly. Jordan seemed preoccupied when he first arrived, but as he said the familiar lines, he relaxed and became Buck. Carley was so accustomed to her lines that she hit every cue. One of her costume changes was rushed, but she got back on stage in time to deliver her line.

Melissa was also preoccupied and missed several cues. Bob had begun to pace along with Chester. Carley wasn't worried. Melissa often gave a faulty performance during the rush week but was flawless once the actual performance started. Evidently Jordan fitted in the same category.

When they got to the scene where Buck was to propose to Alice and kiss her, Carley actually felt herself blushing as Jordan said the words. He had given them a depth of meaning that Chester had never expected, she was sure.

Although she expected the usual peck on the cheek, Jordan surprised her by pulling her into his arms and kissing her as if no one else were around. Carley felt her head spin as he released her, and as she steadied herself against him, she heard the cast applaud.

"Perfect!" Bob shouted from the dim rows of seats. "Perfect! Do it exactly like that during the performances!"

Carley seemed to float through the rest of the scene.

"Wow!" Stacy whispered as she helped Carley dress for the last act. "I think I see what you mean about him!"

Carley smiled.

The farewell lines were difficult. Carley, as Alice, wanted to run into Jordan's arms instead of telling Buck goodbye forever, and although she knew her lines by heart and delivered them word for word, she wasn't convincing.

"Do that part once more," Bob called out. "Just the part staring 'Buck, you've never understood me.' Carley, remember, this jerk wants you pregnant and barefoot for the rest of your life."

Carley chuckled with the rest of the cast, but this time she put her soul into it. When she left the stage she stormed out as if her next stop was New York City.

"Good! Okay, folks, down front for notes!" Bob yelled.

Carley found herself sitting across the stage from Jordan, but she didn't mind. From this angle she could see him better and tantalize herself with expectations of the evening to come.

As soon as Bob finished his wrap-up instructions, Carley changed into her street clothes and put her costumes in order for the technical rehearsal the following night.

Jordan watched her, smiling to himself. She was a good actress, and her voice was superb. Even if he didn't love her, he admired her abilities. He thought of the evening ahead and asked himself for the hundredth time that day if he should tell her he loved her. He had almost done so on several occasions, but had never felt the time was right. Besides, he argued with himself, she must know how he felt. Carley had always been perceptive to all his moods. At times it was almost as if she could read his mind.

And marriage? He wanted Carley—he was sure of that—but he was still wary of marriage. He had seen too many people change when that wedding ring slipped into place. What he and Carley shared now was a slice of heaven. What if the wedding ceremony spoiled it?

Maybe one reason they were so happy was the freedom they each had to walk away. When Jordan married again, he wanted it to be forever. Maybe he was rushing matters to propose so soon. He nodded to himself. He would tell her he loved her; the proposal would wait until later.

Melissa came out of the dressing area and gave him a timorous smile and a wave as she started out the back door. Jordan waved back. He had spent the afternoon washing the vulgarities off her house. He was amazed that she was brave enough to go back there again, but she was reluctant to ask any of her friends for sanctuary.

All at once Melissa ran back in and hurried over to him. Her face was ashen and her hands were shaking so hard that she almost dropped the note she shoved at him.

"Tonight," it said. "You die tonight."

Jordan lifted his eyes from the paper and looked at Melissa.

"It was stuck under the windshield wiper on my car. Jordan, he's going to kill me!" she whispered, unable to control her hysteria.

"Hush, hush," he soothed as he automatically put his arms around her. "It's going to be all right."

Melissa wasn't crying; she was much too frightened for that. Instead she shook from head to toe as if she were having a chill.

Jordan frowned toward the dressing rooms. Melissa had every reason to be scared. He didn't think this was an idle threat. Stacy came out of the dressing room, and when she saw Jordan and Melissa, she stopped and stared. Jordan was suddenly reminded of his plans for the evening, and his heart sank. He hated the thought, but knew he would have to tell Carley he couldn't see her that night or any night until after the play was over and Melissa was safely out of town. This woman couldn't be left in jeopardy.

"Wait here," he told Melissa. "I'll be right back." she nodded silently.

When he entered the dressing room, Carley met him with a radiant smile. "I'm ready," she said.

"I have to cancel our plans for tonight."

"What?" Her smile faded.

"Something has come up. I...well, it's unavoid-able."

"What's wrong?"

"I can't explain. It's related to business."

Carley stared at him. "At eleven o'clock at night?"

"I can't explain." He came to her and kissed her forehead. He didn't trust himself to kiss her lips. All his good intentions might vanish.

"Will I see you tomorrow night?" she asked.

He shook his head. "I'm afraid I'm going to be tied up until the play is over. I'm sorry, Carley. Please try to understand."

She nodded as if she were in shock, and he smiled at her. When all this was over, he said to himself, he would explain it to her. Until then he was glad she was being reasonable.

Jordan went back to Melissa and took her arm. He wasn't sure she was capable of walking without assis-tance. "Are you okay? Can you drive?"

She nodded mutely, then added, "But I can't go home! Jack will break in! He'll—"

"Take it easy. You aren't going to be there. You're coming home with me."

"What?" Her eyes widened with hope.

"I have several extra bedrooms, and Jack will never look for you there. Tomorrow we'll go and get whatever you need for the rest of the week."

"You'd do that for me?"

"We're friends." He smiled and added, "And I have to take care of my clients, don't I? We have a divorce to finalize in a couple of days."

Melissa smiled with relief as Jordan led her past Stacy and out the back door.

Chapter Fourteen

What do you mean, he left with Melissa?"

Stacy nodded, her eyes troubled. "They went right past me. Carley, he had his arm around her."

"I don't believe it!"

"You can ask Bob. He saw them, too."

Carley felt tears sting her eyes, and she turned away and blinked to keep from crying. Taking a deep breath, she said, "Come with me. I'm going to find out what's going on here."

Stacy got in Carley's car, and they drove to Melissa's street and parked a few doors down. "I don't see her car," Carley said. "She isn't here."

"She's had plenty of time to get home. They left before we did."

"Maybe he gave her a ride to rehearsal. Her car stays in the shop half the time."

"I rode with her. I'm sure she had her car tonight. She was supposed to take me home, too."

"You mean she left the theater without seeing to it that you had a ride home?" Carley was shocked that Melissa would be so inconsiderate.

"I guess she forgot."

"Forgot!"

"She's had a lot on her mind, and Jordan is pretty distracting. Besides, she knew you were still there and so was Bob. I could have gotten another ride."

"I think she has behaved abominably!"

"Come on, Carley. You know you're more angry at Melissa for leaving with Jordan than you are because she stranded me."

Carley glared at Melissa's small frame house. She didn't dare voice what she was feeling. If only she hadn't been so talkative earlier! She trusted Stacy not to spread what she had said, but she was embarrassed that she had gushed on about how much she loved Jordan. The scoundrel! She wished she could cut his heart out— if he had one.

"I feel silly sitting here," Carley said at last. "If Melissa was home, we would see her car under the carport and Jordan's would stand out like a snake in a henhouse."

"An apt analogy," Stacy remarked. "I guess you should take me home. Maybe it was business after all."

"As far as I know, Jordan only does business in one place."

They drove downtown and into the empty parking lot by Jordan's law firm. The lot was empty, and the office was dark and locked.

"Maybe I'm wrong about the whole thing," Stacy said. "Let's go home and forget about it."

Carley didn't trust herself to answer. She drove past the hardware store and the soda fountain. Neither Jordan's nor Melissa's car was there.

"Hey, you missed my street," Stacy said. "You're taking me home, remember?"

"We have one more stop first."

She drove through the quiet streets of Apple Tree toward the edge of town with grim determination, afraid of what she'd find when she reached her destination, but compelled to see for herself. As she neared the last in a row of stately old homes, Carley cut off her lights, then turned into Jordan's drive.

"Carley! What are you doing?"

Carley made no reply as she headed around the house to the place in back where she had parked the night before. In the dark she almost rear-ended Melissa's car.

Carley slammed on her brakes and glared at the two cars parked side by side in the inky blackness. Then she looked over at the house. All the lights were out downstairs, but not upstairs. Burning tears brimmed in her eyes and overflowed.

"We've got to get out of here!" Stacy whispered as if she might be overheard. "This is trespassing!"

Carley shoved the gearshift in reverse and turned around. Melissa was there with Jordan. Even now she was upstairs with him. They certainly hadn't wasted any time on small talk! Carley thought of Melissa lying naked in Jordan's big bed in the same place Carley had lain only hours before, and she felt nauseated. How could he do this to her! How had she been so stupid as to trust him again! Especially when she knew Melissa was calling him at home, even twice while Carley was there.

"You know," Carley said in a tight voice, "I never learn. I'm one of those people who has to have a house fall in on her before she will listen."

"Look, maybe there's some explanation..."

"Of course there is. He's sleeping with both of us! Don't look so surprised. You must have suspected that I was with him last night after the way I was carrying on about him this afternoon."

"It's really none of my business and—"

"Well, I was! I was right up there where Melissa is now." Carley yanked on her headlights as she turned onto the street, then slapped her palm on the steering wheel. "I'm so damned mad!"

"I think you should come in for a while when you get to my house. You shouldn't be alone when you're this upset."

"I can't believe I was so stupid! It's not as if Jordan never did anything like this before! He must enjoy the thrill of having two women at his beck and call. Why there may be a whole harem, for all I know."

"Calm down, Carley. We'll have a cup of coffee and talk about it rationally."

"Well, he won't have me on his trotline anymore!" Carley said as if Stacy hadn't spoken. "It's taken me a long time, but I've finally wised up."

"I wish I had never told you he left with Melissa," Stacy said in a miserable voice. "I had no intention of stirring up so much trouble."

"I'm glad you told me. I really am! Otherwise I would have continued making a fool of myself."

"What are you going to do?"

Carley frowned. "I don't know. One thing is for sure—I'm not going to stay in town."

"You're not moving!" Stacy gasped.

"No. At least not yet. But I *am* going on a long vacation. To Europe maybe. Rome! That's it, I'll go to Rome. I haven't been there in years."

"But the play..."

"I know, I know. I have to stay until it's over, but that's only a few days." Carley stopped in front of Stacy's house. "I can leave as soon as the last performance is over."

"I think you're overreacting. All that has happened, really, is that Jordan is with Melissa. He told you it was business. You should at least give him a chance to explain."

"To lie, you mean. I've been upstairs in Jordan's house, and there isn't an office there. Only bedrooms. No, there's no mistake."

"At least come in until you calm down," Stacy reasoned.

"Thanks, but I'm too upset. I'd wake up Bill and Billy."

"I'm worried about you."

"There's really no reason to be. I'm not going to do anything foolish. I'll go home, fix myself a stiff drink and start planning my trip to Rome."

Stacy reluctantly got out and leaned over to say, "Think this over carefully. I still say you're making too much of it."

"I'm not. Not under the circumstances. And I need a vacation. I haven't been away from home for any length of time in years. Don't worry about me."

She waited until Stacy was safely inside her house, then drove away. Rome was just what she needed. And if she came home and Jordan still looked sexy to her, she would travel to China. One of the benefits of being a rich widow was that she didn't have to stay anywhere she didn't want to.

But as she drove home, Carley cried.

Jordan brushed aside his bedroom window curtain and peered into the night. He had been certain he'd heard a car drive up, but he couldn't see anything. Letting the curtain drop back in place, he frowned. Was Jack crazy enough to try to get to Melissa here? Jordan pulled the note out of his pocket and reread it. Jack had scrawled his message to Melissa in pencil on paper he'd torn from a white shopping bag. The phrasing as well as the handwriting indicated a dangerously insane mind.

He put the note in the folder he would take to the police the next day. He would be glad when this unpleasantness was over and Melissa was safely on her way to Dallas.

From the bathroom down the hall, he could hear her brushing her teeth. He had put her in the back room where he was positive she couldn't be seen from the street in case she left her curtains open. Jordan didn't want Jack to have any clue that she was here. Not when Jordan would have to leave her alone while he went to work. If Melissa stayed inside and away from the front windows, she should be safe. Her car couldn't be seen unless someone drove all the way around to the back of the house.

Again he frowned. He had been positive he heard a car a few minutes before. Jordan went out on his balcony and leaned on the railing. The silvery lake was serene, just as it should be. In the moonlight, the lawn was a landscape of pewter with black smudges of trees and bushes. The driveway was empty, and all was quiet.

Just imagination, he told himself. He thought of Carley and wished he was holding her instead of guarding Melissa. He had certainly expected a more pleasurable evening than this. At least Melissa was too frightened of Jack to have any romantic notions he would have to fend off. Jordan wanted Carley and no one else. Yes, he would be glad when he could get Melissa safely out of town and get on with his life.

The technical rehearsal for *Moonbeams and Roses* went slowly, even though there were few special effects required. The man working the new light control board was still familiarizing himself with the new equipment and felt it necessary to try several lighting combinations for each scene before he got the proper atmosphere. Nerves among the cast members were strung tight. Opening night was looming near, and everyone was full of nervous jitters.

"What's the matter with you?" Jordan whispered while they waited for the tech man to discover how to stimulate moonlight.

"I don't want to talk about it."

"Come on, Carley. Don't give me that."

She glared up at him. Despite her good intentions to go home and plan her trip, she had spent most of the night crying and pacing, and she felt terrible. Seeing Jordan and Melissa arrive together had only made it worse.

"I've decided to take a vacation," she said in an undertone that couldn't be overheard by the others. "A long vacation."

"You have? Since when? You never mentioned a vacation to me."

"It was a recent decision, and it should be perfectly obvious to you that neither of us tells the other everything."

"What's that supposed to mean?"

She lifted her chin defiantly as Bob called for them to go over the scene once more.

When they again had a chance to talk, Jordan said, "Now what's this about a vacation?"

"I've decided to go to Rome."

"Rome!"

"Keep your voice down. Yes, Rome."

"Rome, Italy?"

"Is there another one I'd be likely to go to?" she asked acidly.

"Why?"

"I like Rome. Edward and I spent our honeymoon there, and I've always been nostalgic about it."

Carley could see from his expression her barb had hit its mark. "I never knew you had such a fondness for ancient things," he said sarcastically. "Edward and Rome together must have been a real thrill for you."

Anger flared in Carley's eyes, and she had to clench her teeth to keep from screaming at him. "As a matter of fact, it was." She tossed her head and took her place on stage for the next scene.

Jordan managed to be beside her during the next pause. "I don't believe for a minute that you've decided to trip down memory lane at this particular time for no reason at all. What the hell is going on?"

"I happen to know where Melissa spent the night last night." She waited for him to deny it, but he only groaned.

"Who else knows?"

"Just Stacy."

"No one else?"

"We didn't think it was newsworthy enough to put a notice in the paper. Half the female population of Apple Tree has probably slept out there. You should open a bed and breakfast house."

"I should have known that was it. Look, Carley, nothing at all happened."

"No? What a shame. But I don't believe it, and I certainly don't want to talk about it."

"Well, you're going to. I'm telling you, nothing is going on between Melissa and me."

"Give me credit for some intelligence, Jordan! The lights were out downstairs, and the ones upstairs were on."

"So that was you who drove up!"

Carley jerked her eyes away. She hadn't intended to admit that.

"Look, I can't explain it to you now, but if you'll give me a chance—"

"Sorry, my flight leaves Houston Sunday night. That means I'll have to leave town immediately after the last performance to get to the airport on time. I won't be going to the cast party."

"How long is this vacation you have planned?" he demanded.

"I haven't decided yet. Maybe a couple of months. Maybe longer."

"Months!"

"What's wrong, Jordan? Did I steal your thunder? Loving and leaving is usually your trick, isn't it? Well, I was taught by a master." She was thoroughly enjoying his helpless anger. "On closing night when Alice goes out that door, it will be me leaving you." The part of her that wanted revenge was almost enjoying this, while the rest of her was in agony. "I'll have my bags in the car, and when I go out the door and leave you on stage, I'll keep going. You'll have to have the curtain call without me."

"You wouldn't!"

"I will!" She forced a cold smile to her face to cover her anguish and walked away.

Opening night was played to an almost full house, and the audience loved it. News of the electricity between Carley and Jordan on stage spread, and the second night people had to be turned away. Everyone had heard there was more to see here than a play by Chester Goode. The old gossip about how he had left her years before to marry the Wallace girl had been revived, and some had speculated on whether Carley's widowhood had played a part in Jordan's return to Apple Tree.

Carley heard the gossip from all sides. Both Arthur and Betsy came over to demand to know what was going on. Carley refused to answer any questions.

"It's a play, Arthur. That's all it is! Just a play!"

"That's not what they're saying at the beauty shop," Betsy put in. "They say it's scandalous the way you kiss each other onstage."

"It's in the script," Carley said defensively. "It wasn't my idea." That kiss scene was the hardest thing she had ever done, and she wished heartily that she had never tried out for the part or had dropped out when Jordan was cast as Buck.

"I have a good mind to talk to Bob Holton about it," Arthur fumed. "To have him take it out."

"It won't do any good. I've already tried. Besides there is only one more performance."

"Thank goodness," Betsy said as she rolled her eyes upward. "This has been so embarrassing."

"Well, you'll have a respite," Carley said. "I'm leaving for Rome after tonight's performance."

"Rome? Not with Jordan Landry, I hope!" Arthur glared at her.

"Certainly not. I'm going on a vacation. Alone. I'll be gone for at least two months, so I'd like for you to look in on the house from time to time. Abby will be here, of course, and she has your number in case there's an emergency.''

"You never said you were going to start traveling!" Betsy exclaimed.

"It was a rather sudden decision. When I return from Rome, I may go somewhere else. I've spent my whole life in Apple Tree, and I want to spread my wings, as Chester Goode would say.''

Arthur looked at Betsy, and she looked back at him. Carley watched the silent exchange, wondering what was up.

"Carley, this is a bit awkward," Arthur began.

"You know Arthur grew up in this house," Betsy put in.

"The fact is, I've always loved this place," he continued. "As you know, I expected to inherit it someday—before Father married you, that is. Carley, what I'm trying to say is, will you sell this house to us?''

"Sell my house?" Carley said doubtfully. "I'm only going on vacation, Arthur.''

"I know, but if you're going to start traveling—and you should, you know, while you're young enough to enjoy it—there's no reason for the house to sit empty.''

"Sell my house?" she repeated. That sounded so permanent!

"We could trade houses," Betsy suggested with excitement. "Ours is really too small for us now that Eddie and Rosalie are growing up. They're so popular that we always have kids simply everywhere. Why, this could be an answer for all of us.''

"I'm not so sure, I . . .''

"Just say you'll think about it," Arthur urged. "We don't want to pressure you. Naturally if you decide to trade houses, we'll pay you the difference in cash.''

"And bear in mind that ours has recently been redecorated," Betsy added. "And you wouldn't have such a large lawn to keep up."

Carley shook her head. "I can't make a decision of this magnitude without consideration. I know this was your home, Arthur, but it's been mine for years. And I like your house, Betsy, but I never considered whether I would like to have it for my own."

"We aren't trying to rush you," Arthur said, all but rubbing his hands together with glee. "We would never have mentioned it if you hadn't decided to start traveling."

Betsy nodded eagerly. "You can give us your answer after you return from Rome. No rush. No rush at all."

Carley saw them out and leaned against the door as she considered their offer. This house was pretty, especially now that she had replaced Edward's beige and tan neutrals with her pastel colors. The house was filled with light through its many windows and the wall of glass blocks. She knew it was much too large for only one person and she was often nervous in it at night, but she would be equally alone in any other house.

Carley closed her eyes. If only it had worked out with Jordan. She was tired of being alone. And she loved him. In spite of everything, regardless of all he had done, she loved him and she missed him.

She went upstairs and finished packing her makeup into her suitcase. Stacy could gather up her stage makeup and costumes for her. After wearing those dresses on stage every night for a week, she wasn't eager to wear them again anytime soon. She was determined to leave as quickly as she could. So far she had managed to avoid or ignore Jordan except on stage, but she didn't trust herself indefinitely.

She closed the suitcase and locked it. Stacy had told her Melissa's divorce had become final Friday afternoon, and Carley assumed Jordan and Melissa had had a grand celebration. Melissa had been at Jordan's house every night. Carley knew, because she had forced herself to drive by Melissa's house after every performance to see if her car was there. Each time it hurt her more, but each time it firmed her resolve to get Jordan out of her life. Now if she could only get him out of her heart.

Carley carried her bags out to the car and put them in the trunk. She would get to the theater early as she had the three previous nights, and would be dressed and in makeup before Melissa arrived with Jordan. While everyone else prepared for the performance, Carley would go over her lines in the back of the auditorium. This way she didn't have to see or speak either to Jordan or Melissa until they were on stage.

As the time neared for the last performance, tension backstage built like wildfire. Melissa was in tears off and on and had to reapply her makeup twice. Jordan couldn't find Carley at all. She somehow never appeared until time for her entrance. He had called her a number of times over the past several days, but her maid had told him she was out, and Carley had either not gotten his messages to call back, or more likely she was still angry. Jordan was becoming frantic.

The divorce had gone smoothly. Jack had stayed away from the courtroom, and Melissa's mother had surprised her by driving down. After Melissa explained to her mother about Jack's threats, they both agreed that staying at Jordan's house until the play was over was best. Then, as soon as the play ended, she and Melissa planned to leave for Dallas. Jordan was looking forward to having his house to himself again.

But was Carley leaving, too? She had said she was, but he had not been able to talk to her about it. He had tried to pump Stacy for information, but she was as cold to him as Carley was and wouldn't tell him anything at all. Jordan could only assume she was going to leave as she had said. He had no idea when, or even if, she would return.

Bob came backstage to tell the cast the auditorium doors were opening and that there was another sellout crowd in the lobby. Chester was so nervous that he was all but trotting as he paced in the wings.

Jordan looked across the empty stage and saw Carley, dressed as Alice, behind the side curtain. When she saw him look her way, she pointedly turned her back.

Jordan had never felt such frustrated anger. He loved her, dammit, and she wouldn't let him tell her so. "I have to talk to you," he whispered to her.

She glared at him over her shoulder and jerked her thumb toward the outer curtain.

"Hush!" Chester said frantically. "The audience will hear you!"

Jordan growled, but he knew they were right. The building's acoustics were perfect. And he couldn't go to her with the curtain about to rise.

Carley's throat felt tight, and her stomach fluttered nervously. This time it was more than her usual flurry of stage fright. Tonight was the last night she would see Jordan. She tried to tell herself she was glad, but inside she already mourned his loss.

Unexpectedly Stacy came running up to Carley. "Carley, I have to tell you something."

"I can't talk now," Carley whispered. "The curtain is about to go up."

"But this is really important. I just talked to Melissa, and she says there's nothing going on between Jordan and herself."

"What?" Carley saw the stage manager step to the curtain pull.

"That's right. It's all a misunderstanding."

Carley wanted to ask a dozen questions, but there was no time. Melissa might think nothing was going on between herself and Jordan, but that said nothing about how Jordan felt about Melissa. And even if it were true that Jordan wasn't romantically involved with Melissa, it didn't matter, for she was sure he didn't care about her, either. She wanted to cry out in frustration, but as the curtain pulleys began to creak, she pushed aside her thoughts and feelings.

Anxiously she reread her first line, then tossed her worn script onto the small table backstage. As the curtain opened, a hush fell over the packed auditorium. Drawing a deep breath, she stepped out onto the stage to deliver her opening line. The spontaneous applause at her entrance bolstered her spirits, and when the applause died down, Alice began to speak.

Backstage, Chester rubbed his hands over and over. "It's a good crowd. Yes, yes, it's a good crowd," he murmured in a low voice.

Jordan ignored him. Unless he did something to stop Carley, she was going to fly off to Rome, and he might never see her again. Even if she did return to Apple Tree, it would be months. Jordan didn't want that. He loved her. He wanted to marry her.

The idea startled him. Marriage? He waited, expecting the usual sense of dread. Instead he felt a growing elation. He loved Carley. Of course he wanted to marry her! He had been a fool not to realize it before now.

On cue he went on stage and to his surprise he received the same ovation as Carley. She stood waiting for him to deliver his lines, a smile pasted on her face.

Jordan didn't know what to do. The play was progressing smoothly, but he had no time at all to speak to her privately. They both gave their lines and moved on cue, but it was Alice and Buck, not Carley and Jordan. Between acts Carley pulled her vanishing act, and Jordan was left pacing and fuming.

The last act began. When he reached the kissing scene, he put everything he had into it. As he bent for the kiss, he paused for the space of a breath and looked deep into her eyes, but saw only anger. Then he drew her into his embrace and kissed her with all the love in his heart. The audience went wild; Carley kept her lips shut.

The last scene began to unfold. Jordan felt panic rising as the lines carried him inextricably toward its conclusion. He loved her! He might never see her again! Only Jordan and possibly Stacy knew that Carley didn't even intend to stay for the curtain call.

Alice picked up the suitcase and crossed to the door on stage left; Buck watched her helplessly from center stage. This was it. The goodbye scene. The moment he had dreaded.

"'I've made my decision, Buck,'" Carley was saying. "'I have to try my wings. To taste life. I have to see what I can be and what I can accomplish without you.'" She lifted her head regally. "'You've done all in your power to keep me here and to mold me in the image you envision for me,'" she said in ringing tones, "'but I've had enough. I'm leaving, Buck. I'm leaving you and I'm leaving this town and I don't want to see either again.'"

In the wings Bob was grinning, and Chester was silently mouthing the words along with the actors.

"'But, Alice...'"

"'Don't try to stop me. This is goodbye!'" She turned on her heels to flounce out the door and out of his life.

"Wait!" Jordan pleaded as he stepped toward her, his hand outstretched. "Don't go!"

Carley faltered. This wasn't in the script! She looked back at him.

"Don't go," he repeated. "Not until you've heard what I have to say. I love you."

Carley's eyes widened. What was happening? She looked at Bob and saw his smile frozen in place. He leaned toward Chester who was frantically shaking his head.

"I said I love you," Jordan repeated. "I mean that. I've wanted to say this to you for a long time. First I was afraid to admit it, then you wouldn't let me near enough to say it. I love you."

A murmur ran through the actors backstage, and Bob made quieting motions with both hands. Chester seemed to be on the verge of apoplexy.

"I...I have to go," Carley stammered. "My life...my life lies ahead of me."

Jordan stepped closer. "No. Your life lies here. With me. Marry me."

"What!" she exclaimed.

Bob threw up his hands and sat down on a pile of rope. Chester looked as if he wanted to strangle someone. All the other actors were staring at the stage, their mouths agape. Out of the corner of her eye Carley saw Melissa grinning from ear to ear. Could it be...?

"I'm asking you to be my wife," Jordan said quietly. "To share all our dreams and our futures. To fill that house with happy children. For us to watch all our sunsets from that gazebo.''

Carley felt as if she were about to faint. That was Jordan talking to her, not Buck to Alice!

Slowly she put down the suitcase and stepped toward him. "I love you. I've always loved you."

Jordan's eyes were tender as he closed the space between them and took both her hands. "I'll always be true to you. Will you marry me?''

Faintly Carley nodded. Then more forcefully she said, "Yes. Yes, I'll marry you!''

Jordan swept her up in his arms and whirled her around as the audience went wild. Amid a standing ovation they kissed with all the passion in their hearts.

Chester wrestled away the boy who was supposed to close the curtain, and he yanked it closed with frenzied movements.

Carley and Jordan paid him no attention at all. They were caught up in their own version of happily ever after.

*   *   *   *   *

"GIVE YOUR HEART TO SILHOUETTE" SWEEPSTAKES
OFFICIAL RULES

NO PURCHASE NECESSARY TO ENTER OR RECEIVE A PRIZE

1. To enter and join the Silhouette Reader Service, rub off the concealment device on all game tickets. This will reveal the potential value for each Sweepstakes entry number and the number of free book(s) you will receive. Accepting the free book(s) will automatically entitle you to also receive a free bonus gift. If you do not wish to take advantage of our introduction to the Silhouette Reader Service but wish to enter the Sweepstakes only, rub off the concealment device on tickets #1-3 only. To enter, return your entire sheet of tickets. Incomplete and/or inaccurate entries are not eligible for that section or section (s) of prizes. Not responsible for mutilated or unreadable entries or inadvertent printing errors. Mechanically reproduced entries are null and void.

2. Either way, your Sweepstakes numbers will be compared against the list of winning numbers generated at random by computer. In the event that all prizes are not claimed, random drawings will be made from all entries received from all presentations to award all unclaimed prizes. All cash prizes are payable in U.S. funds. This is in addition to any free, surprise or mystery gifts that might be offered. The following prizes are awarded in this sweepstakes:

(1)	*Grand Prize	$1,000,000	Annuity
(1)	First Prize	$35,000	
(1)	Second Prize	$10,000	
(3)	Third Prize	$5,000	
(10)	Fourth Prize	$1,000	
(25)	Fifth Prize	$500	
(5000)	Sixth Prize	$5	

*The Grand Prize is payable through a $1,000,000 annuity. Winner may elect to receive $25,000 a year for 40 years, totaling up to $1,000,000 without interest, or $350,000 in one cash payment. Winners selected will receive the prizes offered in the Sweepstakes promotion they receive.
Entrants may cancel the Reader Service privileges at any time without cost or obligation to buy (see details in center insert card).

3. Versions of this Sweepstakes with different graphics may be offered in other mailings or at retail outlets by Torstar Corp. and its affiliates. This promotion is being conducted under the supervision of Marden-Kane, Inc., an independent judging organization. By entering this Sweepstakes, each entrant accepts and agrees to be bound by these rules and the decisions of the judges, which shall be final and binding. Odds of winning are dependent upon the total number of entries received. Taxes, if any, are the sole responsibility of the winners. Prizes are nontransferable. All entries must be received by March 31, 1990. The drawing will take place on April 30, 1990, at the offices of Marden-Kane, Inc., Lake Success, N.Y.

4. This offer is open to residents of the U.S., Great Britain and Canada, 18 years or older, except employees of Torstar Corp., its affiliates, and subsidiaries, Marden-Kane, Inc. and all other agencies and persons connected with conducting this Sweepstakes. All federal, state and local laws apply. Void wherever prohibited or restricted by law.

5. Winners will be notified by mail and may be required to execute an affidavit of eligibility and release that must be returned within 14 days after notification. Canadian winners will be required to answer a skill-testing question. Winners consent to the use of their name, photograph and/or likeness for advertising and publicity in conjunction with this and similar promotions without additional compensation. One prize per family or household.

6. For a list of our most current major prizewinners, send a stamped, self-addressed envelope to: WINNERS LIST, c/o MARDEN-KANE, INC., P.O. BOX 701, SAYREVILLE, N.J. 08871

If Sweepstakes entry form is missing, please print your name and address on a 3" x 5" piece of plain paper and send to:

In the U.S.	In Canada
Sweepstakes Entry	Sweepstakes Entry
901 Fuhrmann Blvd.	P.O. Box 609
P.O. Box 1867	Fort Erie, Ontario
Buffalo, NY 14269-1867	L2A 5X3

LTY-S69R

You'll flip . . . your pages won't!
Read paperbacks *hands-free* with

Book Mate·I

The perfect "mate" for all your romance paperbacks

Traveling • Vacationing • At Work • In Bed • Studying • Cooking • Eating

Perfect size for all standard paperbacks, this wonderful invention makes reading a pure pleasure! Ingenious design holds paperback books OPEN and FLAT so even wind can't ruffle pages — leaves your hands free to do other things. Reinforced, wipe-clean vinyl-covered holder flexes to let you turn pages without undoing the strap . . . supports paperbacks so well, they have the strength of hardcovers!

Pages turn WITHOUT opening the strap.

SEE-THROUGH STRAP

Reinforced back stays flat.

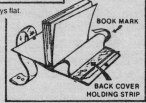

Built in bookmark.

BOOK MARK

BACK COVER HOLDING STRIP

10˝ x 7¼˝, opened.
Snaps closed for easy carrying, too.

Available now. Send your name, address, and zip code, along with a check or money order for just $5.95 + .75¢ for postage & handling (for a total of $6.70) payable to Reader Service to:

Reader Service
Bookmate Offer
901 Fuhrmann Blvd.
P.O. Box 1396
Buffalo, N.Y. 14269-1396

Offer not available in Canada
* New York and Iowa residents add appropriate sales tax.

BM-G

COMING NEXT MONTH

#535 NO SURRENDER—Lindsay McKenna
Navy pilot Alyssa Trayhern's assignment with arrogant jet jockey
Clay Cantrell threatens her pride, her career—and her heart—with a
crash landing. Book Two of Lindsay McKenna's gripping LOVE
AND GLORY series.

#536 A TENDER SILENCE—Karen Keast
Former POW Kell Chaisson knew all about survival. He'd brave
Bangkok's dangers to help Anne Elise Butler trace her MIA
husband's fate, but would he survive loving another man's wife?

#537 THORNE'S WIFE—Joan Hohl
Jonas Thorne was accomplished, powerful, devastatingly attractive.
Valerie Thorne loved her husband, but what would it take to convince
domineering Jonas that she was a person, not simply his wife?

#538 LIGHT FOR ANOTHER NIGHT—Anne Lacey
Wildlife biologist Brittany Hagen loved the wolves on primeval Isle
Svenson . . . until she encountered the two-legged variety—in the
person of ferociously attractive, predatory Paul Johnson.

#539 EMILY'S HOUSE—Nikki Benjamin
Vowing to secretly support widowed Emily Anderson and her child,
Major Joseph Cortez rented rooms in her house. But, hiding a guilty
secret, could he ever gain entrance to Emily's heart?

#540 LOVE THIS STRANGER—Linda Shaw
Pregnant nutritionist Mary Smith unwittingly assumed another
woman's identity when she accepted a job with the Olympic ski team.
Worse, she also "inherited" devastating Dr. Jed Kilpatrick—the
other woman's lover!
